Soul Switchers

Part 1

Habent Sua Fata Libelli

Manhanset House
Shelter Island Hts., New York 11965-0342

bricktower@aol.com • tech@absolutelyamazingebooks.com
• absolutelyamazingebooks.com

Mentor Books is a joint imprint of
Absolutely Amazing eBooks
and AdLab Media Communications, LLC.

The Absolutely Amazing eBooks colophon is a trademark of
J. T. Colby & Company, Inc.

Library of Congress Cataloging-in-Publication Data
Cohen, Barry H.
Soul Switchers.
p. cm.
1. FICTION / Science Fiction / Time Travel 2. FICTION / Science Fiction / Crime.
3. FICTION / Thrillers / Suspense
Fiction, I. Title.
ISBN: 978-1-955036-33-7, Trade Paper

Cover Design: Samantha Fury

July 2022

Soul Switchers

Part 1

a novel by

Barry H. Cohen

Dedication:
To the giants of science fiction who forged the path.

Table of Contents

Chapter I

1966

Jenny Crawford slowly awoke, her eyelids still pasted together. Gently rubbing them, her vision began to clear. The familiar and pleasant smell of her freshly painted walls greeted her. She had chosen her favorite color, bright yellow. Sunlight had just begun to pierce the sheer brown curtains as they gently billowed in the early autumn breeze. She always preferred to remain in touch with the world outdoors.

With one deft move, Jenny swung both legs out from under the blanket and the top sheet. Her feet touched down gently as she became acutely aware of the sensation of the slightly rough carpet. Checking the alarm clock, she noted the time: 6:36. She could have slept longer, but she chose not to. With a purposeful gait, Jenny paraded into the bathroom. Another sensation struck her acutely as the soles of her feet slid across the smooth, cool tile floor. She hardly paid attention to the face staring back at her in the mirror. She had more important things to do.

In one swift move, Jenny let her night gown fall to the floor. She reached for the faucets, taking care not to make the water excessively hot. Before she could test it, she heard a loud thud on the floor of the apartment above her. She had learned long ago to ignore such noises. It had become the standard for urban living. Jenny resumed her entry into the shower. The tepid water flooded over her. Once again, she experienced a heightened level of sensation. Luxuriating, she slowly rotated as if to dance. The high pressure water bounced off of her like bullets. Gradually, she became oblivious to the stinging sensation. As she let the bar of soap in her hand glide across her body, she felt a pleasurable twinge—almost a forbidden pleasure. Secretly, she craved more. Jenny seldom indulged herself in physical pleasure. She considered herself a more spiritual person. It just seemed out of character to her. No matter. She dismissed the thought as she turned the squeaking faucets off. The large drops of water continued to cascade into the drain, slowly emptying the pipe.

Clearing her eyes, Jenny threw back her wet hair and seized the towel from the rack on the back of the bathroom door. Everything seemed so familiar—and somehow, not. She grabbed a second towel from the other rack—the rusty one, and flung it over her head, vigorously draining the excess water from her hair. A certain excitement permeated her being—as if she somehow sensed that the day held wondrous things yet to unfold. It was all about the knowing for Jenny. She craved knowledge at every turn.

With the few extra minutes she gained by waking earlier, Jenny reviewed the morning newspaper retrieved from her doorstep, eying the neighbor's black cat. Never superstitious, she nonetheless swiftly closed the door on the would-be interloper as it hissed and showed teeth. She suddenly recalled a fearful encounter she had as a young child. Jenny and her brothers helped a neighbor move. Their cat sat on her lap in the rented truck. The extreme heat must have aggravated the cat. It dug its claws into her thighs. In self-defense, she flung the cat to the floor of the truck. It rebounded, landing squarely back on her lap. At eight years old, it frightened her. She had forgotten about it until that moment. Refocusing her attention on the morning news, Jenny snatched the freshly brewed cup of coffee. The aroma wafted its way into her nostrils, waking her senses. Bad news. The war in Viet Nam continued to heat up. America ratcheted up its efforts. Advisors, they called them. Jenny usually didn't pay much attention to politics and government. They didn't affect her life much, she thought. Another thud on the floor of the apartment above. She tossed the newspaper aside on the kitchen table and returned to the bathroom. In minutes, she found herself staring into her bedroom closet. Most of the time Jenny dressed conservatively, but well. Today, something stirred inside of her. A certain craving nibbled at her as she downed the last of her now much cooled coffee. She withdrew the red dress and red shoes from the closet. It suited her mood.

Minutes later, Jenny raised the garage door behind her apartment building. Her brand new 1966 Ford Mustang glistened in the morning sun. The engine roared. The car smoothly took to the road. Jenny adjusted the radio dial as she pulled up to the red light. The newscaster interrupted the disk jockey's patter. More talk of war. Most Americans couldn't even find Viet Nam on a map. Jenny changed the station, opting for classical music. Her parents met when they both played for an orchestra. Their home always had classical or opera music playing. It permeated the family's bloodline all the way back to England, generations before. The music put Jenny at ease—almost too much. She jerked the wheel as the car in front of her made a panic stop to avoid a child crossing the street. Near death experiences seemed to surround Jenny. She often wondered about that. Regaining her composure, she pulled into the parking lot of her office building.

Climbing the stairs of the old professional building, Jenny watched as the workmen re-tiled the foyer floor below her. She glanced down. Just at that moment, she nearly bumped into an unfamiliar figure, an older man ambling his way along the wall. She thought about asking him if he needed help but decided at the last minute not to. Then, she froze in her tracks. He reminded her so much of her late father. Or did he? Could she have imagined it? Too dark to tell. She tried not to stare but couldn't help herself. He seemed as though he tried to attract her attention—like he attempted to speak, but no words came out. Jenny quickly spun around and left him behind.

The sign on her door read, "Jen Crawford, PhD, Counseling Psychologist." The key in the door, Jenny swung it open. Something seemed amiss. She couldn't put her finger on it. Seeing nothing out of place, she shuttled over to her desk. Her father had taught her the trick of leaving a dollar bill in plain sight. If it was missing, she was taught not to enter. She threw caution to the wind that day. The usual musty smell permeated the office. She switched on the overhead lights and then her desk lamp. Throwing the window open, she noticed a scratching sound in the ceiling. Squirrels, mice, perhaps even rats often made their home in buildings like this. Nothing to worry about. She glanced out the window as the buses and trucks roared by on the other side of the playground that separated her office building from the school. No sign of children that morning. They must have taken a field trip.

Jenny reviewed her open appointment book. As much as she loved her work and truly believed she helped people, at times she felt like a human sponge, soaking up others' misery and worry. How do you expel that? In graduate school, they taught her she must do just that. You could have empathy, but you needed to keep a certain distance—a wall between yourself and your patients' trauma—or risk getting sucked into their vortexes. She scanned the books on the shelf above her desk. Dust webs had begun to form. She blew them off. The scratching sound resumed, this time in the wall rather than the ceiling. Jenny's curiosity got the better of her. She cracked the office door and peaked through the narrow opening, half expecting to see the old man out there. She did. He looked as though he had written on the peeling walls with his finger. If only she could tell what he wanted to express. She pulled back and retreated into the office. She needed another cup of coffee. Jenny busied herself with the coffee pot, trying to put the forlorn figure out of her mind. She needed to focus her attention on her work. Her first session would begin soon. She opened the heavy filing cabinet drawer and withdrew a manila folder, placing it on her desk. It bore the name "Jeffrey Clyman."

Jenny pored over Jeffrey Clyman's file, each hand-written note triggering a recall of her sessions. He had sought her out on the advice of his ex-girlfriend, who felt his problems began to overtake the momentum of their floundering relationship. Jeffrey worked as a legal assistant while pursuing the study of law at night. He preferred to believe he simply struggled with a stressful routine but acquiesced and decided to squeeze the therapy sessions into his already tight schedule. Jenny secretly admitted to herself that she found Jeffrey attractive. However, she would never slip out of the role of a therapist and cross the line to fraternize with a patient. Jenny jerked her head up with a start, suddenly noticing Jeffrey standing over her desk.

"Sorry. I didn't mean to scare you. The door was open."

Jenny motioned for him to sit on the couch and offered him coffee.

"No, thanks. I just had some, Dr. Crawford."

They studied one another, making sure not to engage in direct eye contact.

Jenny sat back in her chair, swiveling to just the right angle. She wanted to glance at Jeffrey from time to time without making it obvious. She noticed him continuing to scope her out—not in a threatening way, but in a curious way. Just as any two animals circle one another, the doctor and her patient seemed to size each other up. Jeffrey let out a sigh and slumped down into the soft leather couch's deep padding. Jenny now leaned in and addressed him in an authoritative, yet consoling tone.

"Jeffrey, let's revisit our last conversation, when you were telling me about your relationship with Donna. Do you remember what you said?"

"Yes, doctor; I remember. I just don't want to talk about Donna," Jeffrey let the words fall listlessly from his lips.

"What do you think would happen if you did talk about Donna, Jeffrey?" Jenny countered.

"It would bring up painful memories of how things went bad and of the break-up," Jeffrey almost stammered, feeling the sting of the thoughts in the pit of his stomach.

"Do you think that facing that pain might help you get past it?" Jenny offered in a conciliatory gesture.

"I'm not sure the pain would lessen or go away; it just hurts, so what's the use?" Jeffrey's voice began to show irritation.

"Jeffrey, sometimes dealing with the very things we find most uncomfortable will move us past them. Are you willing to confront the pain?" Jenny began to probe.

"I don't know, Doctor Crawford. It almost *haunts* me sometimes—like something I just can't shake off. I know it was my fault. I never gave her enough attention," Jeffrey admitted.

"Now, that's good progress. You're looking the problem square in the eye. Acknowledge yourself for that. But don't be too rough on yourself. On the one hand, you had a busy schedule, but on the other hand, you may not have made enough of an effort to find time to include Donna in your life. Does that make sense to you?" Jenny pulled her chair forward to lock in his gaze.

Jeffrey paused to think about her words. Finally, he spoke.

"Okay. But can we talk about something else?"

"Go on. What's on your mind, Jeffrey?

"I've been having dreams—really vivid ones. They disturb me. They don't exactly scare me or wake me up. They just leave me puzzled. When I wake up, I feel like they were real and like they're going to continue. I know I'm awake and I know I was asleep when I had them, but they kind of gnaw at me," Jeff related in a pained voice.

"That's perfectly normal, Jeff. You see, dreams are a sort of workshop for the mind, where we can resolve the problems that plague us during our waking life. Would you care to share any of these dreams?" Jenny queried.

"Yes, I can do that. There's one I keep having. I'm in a building—it might be this one, and I feel like I'm being followed. I keep looking around, but I don't see anyone. Then, when I turn around, I come face to face with a man."

"Do you know this man—is he familiar to you?" Jenny inquired, running her fingers around the pen on her desk.

"No, he's not anyone I know or have ever seen. He doesn't exactly scare me, but he makes me uncomfortable," Jeffrey's voice cracked as he answered.

"Can you describe him for me? Sometimes the figures in dreams represent real people in our lives. They just may not look like them," Jenny responded as she gestured in the air with the pen.

"Okay. He's an older man; about my height, but a little bent over. He looks a bit unkempt and disheveled—he needs a haircut and a shave. He has gold rimmed glasses and he wears a raincoat. That's all I remember about him."

Inwardly, Jenny felt a jolt pass through her. He had described the man she saw in the hallway this morning.

"So, what does this man do or say that seems to upset you?" Jenny dug a little deeper.

"I'm not really sure. He doesn't speak. He just walks along. He seems to sort of hug the wall. In last night's dream, he looked like he had written something on the wall, but there was nothing there."

Jenny began to feel a tightness in her throat. She became aware that the two of them somehow had a shared vision. Her curiosity overtook her momentarily as she realized she had begun to probe more for her own self satisfaction than to help her patient. She concealed her feelings. Jenny glanced over at the clock on the wall.

"Well, we've run out of time. I feel you're making definite progress. How do you feel?"

"Better, Dr. Crawford, definitely better. Should I come the same time next week?"

Jenny opened the appointment book on her desk, thumbing through the pages.

"Yes, that would be fine."

She rose from her desk and escorted him to the door, half expecting to see the old man still shuffling down the hallway. She darted a glance in either direction. No one in sight. She watched Jeffrey as he briskly descended the stairs and disappeared from view. Jenny discarded her now cold cup of coffee and poured another, sinking into her chair. She knew she should prepare for her next session, but the strange connection between her patient's dream and her own waking encounter plagued her. Unable to slough it off, she focused intently on it, making a note in the diary she kept in the back of her appointment book. She had past experiences where writing down any occurrences with a deep emotional impact would eventually take shape in a pattern where she might discern some meaning later. The act seemed to relieve her. It was done—at least for now.

The remaining sessions of the day seemed uneventful for Jenny, to say the least—a husband riddled with guilt over a one-time unfaithful encounter while traveling alone on business out of town; a housewife bored and slipping into an alcohol habit; a low-level politician conflicted over a minor infraction. Jenny poured her heart and soul into every patient's therapy session, but somehow, only Jeffrey Clyman's seemed important on this day. By the end of the day, Jenny felt emotionally tired—somehow more drained than usual. The vision of the man in the hallway and the parallel to Jeffrey's recurring dream haunted her. She couldn't shake it off. Finally, she finished compiling her notes and filed away each patient's folder, except Jeffrey's. She stared at it, opened it, re-read the day's session notes, then flipped back to her journal notes, comparing the two. They matched exactly. Jenny closed Jeffrey's folder and filed it away, closed her journal, flipped off the light switch and unplugged the coffee pot. She picked up her purse, locked the office door and left.

The sky over Elizabethtown had already become dusky. Leaves fell from the trees in the park across the street and swirled around Jenny as she approached her car in the parking lot. She turned the key and the engine roared. With a quick glance in the rear-view mirror, Jenny began to back the car out of her parking space. She hit the brake abruptly as she spied the figure suddenly appearing behind the car. She waited. Looking over her shoulder, she saw no one and proceeded on her way. Her heart pounded; her breathing accelerated. She knew she saw him, if only for an instant.

Jenny entered her apartment with caution, darting glances in every direction, still expecting to see the man. She saw no one. Her next-door neighbor waved to her. An older widow, Kay had lived alone in the apartment for many years. She felt comforted whenever Jenny returned, just knowing someone was there. Kay remained respectful of Jenny's privacy. She seldom stopped to talk to her, she almost never rang her doorbell and she had never even entered Jenny's apartment. Relieved just to have privacy, Jenny kicked off her high heels and sank into the easy chair in the living room. No sooner did she pick up a magazine from the coffee table then she had a premonition that the phone would ring. It did. She ambled into the kitchen and answered the wall phone on the third ring. She heard nothing.

As she stood there, Jenny became aware of her hunger. Just then she remembered that she had skipped lunch and only eaten an apple between sessions. She looked around the kitchen, rifling through cabinets and the refrigerator to see what she could cobble together for dinner. Admittedly, she hadn't paid much attention to cuisine. Food simply didn't excite her much. Eventually, she managed to re-heat the thawed chicken parts that lay in the refrigerator. Television never interested her much either. She thought about calling a friend, but most of her friends had moved away and settled in other cities after college. Too early to sleep, Jenny settled back into the living room chair with the magazine. She thumbed through the pages of the *National Geographic*, imagining the lives of the people in sub-Saharan Africa—how they struggled each day to find food and water, to fight off disease and watched their children die before their eyes—while people in our part of the world decided how big a house to buy, which car to buy and what college their children should attend. Somehow it didn't seem right to Jenny. Then again, only a few years had passed since America had passed the Civil Rights Act, assuring equal rights for people of color. She thought about it. While we had advanced with technology, were we any farther ahead of the rest of the world morally and ethically?

Probably not. As much as she tried to leave work behind her when she came home, Jenny couldn't help but think about today's unusual occurrences. She wondered whether she dwelled on them too much because she had become so socially isolated. Perhaps she needed other interests to keep her occupied in her spare time. Once again, she had a premonition that the phone would ring. It did. This time she hesitated, thinking that if it was a wrong number, maybe they would hang up. They didn't. It rang and rang. After the twelfth ring, she reluctantly answered it. Jenny let our a sigh of relief as she heard her mother's voice.

"Yes, mother, I'm fine. I know. I should call you more often. More importantly, how are you?"

Jenny knew if she switched the focus away from herself, her mother would stop the embarrassing probing, which she considered prying, into her life.

"Yes, the neighborhood is safe enough."

Once again, the focus shifted back to Jenny's life.

"Yes, I get out on weekends. I prefer not to go out on week nights, when I have to get up early the next morning. I really need to go now; I promised I would help my next door neighbor with her check book."

Jenny couldn't help but slip in a little white lie. Sometimes she needed to disengage. As the evening wore on, Jenny felt a funk slipping over her. Eventually, she succumbed to sleep. The dreams came on one after another, like a series of films flashed across a screen. The last of them disturbed her.

"Jeffrey, what are you doing in my apartment? You know you can't come here. You don't belong here. I'm not even dressed."

"Shhhh; it's all right. I would never harm you. I'm here to protect you," Jeffrey whispered.

He slipped his arms around her waist. She didn't stop him. He drew closer. They lay on the bed. She noticed his arousal, followed by her own. He ran his hands the length of her legs. She grabbed his hand and thrust it between her legs. The excitement surged through her body. She opened her eyes as he leaned over her. She sprang up, seeing the figure of the old man standing behind Jeffrey. Then she awoke to the empty room. A shaft of sunlight penetrated the curtains as they began to billow in the breeze.

An entire week of Jenny's life seemed to evaporate. The dreams did not repeat, but she held onto them in her head, searching for meaning. She entered them in her diary and continued to review them, but she felt blocked. She could much more easily interpret her patients' dreams than her own. One detail came back to her during the course of the week. While she stood in line at the coffee shop, she spied a man with a tattoo on his arm. In an instant, she recalled seeing a similar marking on the man in the dream. It vaguely resembled two letter "S's" entwined together. As she thought about it more, the characters more closely resembled two serpents or maybe sea horses interlaced. Jenny searched the books on her office bookcase for standard symbols but could not find anything like it.

Finally, Thursday rolled around. She looked forward to the day with both a glimmer of excitement and trepidation. Jeffrey Clyman had his session that day. Jenny did the usual preparation. Something seemed out of the ordinary. Jeffrey's demeanor confirmed it. He entered the office as if his presence there required him to overcome a great fear. Jenny sensed it immediately. This time he accepted her offer of coffee as he removed his jacket and slowly sat on the edge of the couch. He appeared tense and even more reserved than usual. Jenny immediately picked up on his discomfort and attempted to put him at ease.

"Jeffrey, you know when you come here, you are in a safe place. You can tell me anything you want. Shall we pick up where we left off last week?" she queried.

"No, Dr. Crawford. I have new concerns troubling me. I need to confront them now," Jeffrey openly admitted.

Jenny remembered her dream. She made every attempt to keep her composure and maintain her professionalism. Still, the dream continued to eat away at her. Still on the edge of the couch, clutching his coffee cup, Jeffrey's hand began to tremble. His lip began to quiver before he spoke. After a long pause and a scan of the room, he spoke.

"Dr. Crawford, I've had disturbing dreams. But this time it was different. You were there. And so was that man—you know, the one I told you about."

Jenny looked up with a start.

"Go on."

"Well, it's kind of embarrassing. I don't know how much detail I should go into—"

"Everything. Tell me all of it."

Jenny uncharacteristically cut him off. Once again, she realized she had probed for her own selfish reasons more than to help her patient unburden himself.

"Well, you and I—we, uh; we got close; I don't know how or why, but we were in bed together. I'm sorry. I don't mean to offend you or to scare you. I don't know how it happened, but it was just a dream," Jeffrey blurted out.

Jenny was anything but offended. She was too shocked by the similarity to her own dream. She once again made an effort to regain her composure and project her professionalism.

"Jeffrey, there is a phenomenon in psychology we call transference. It involves transferring feelings we have for one person onto another. The therapist is often the object of this transference. You simply have to determine who the object of your affection might have been. And I'm not the least bit offended. What else do you feel comfortable sharing with me about the dream?" Jenny asked.

"Here's the part that really confused me. That man was there, too. The one I told you about. He watched us," Jeffrey stammered.

Jenny drew herself forward, picked up the pen from her desk set, pointed in the air with it and entreated him to continue.

"What else do you remember? Did you recognize the location, were there any colors you remember or any other details about this man?" Jenny urged him to think harder.

"This time I had a feeling that I knew him or should know him, even though I don't recognize his face. He nodded to me as if he knew me. I did notice one thing. Remember how I told you last week that he seemed to write on the hallway walls outside your office? Well, I think I know what he wrote," Jeffrey continued in a somewhat calmer voice, now at ease.

"And what did he write?"

"I think it was 'S S', Dr. Crawford."

Jenny dropped the pen.

"Well, we'll have to do some digging to figure out what that might mean for you, Jeffrey. You see, while there are certain symbols that are universal in dreams, two people can have a similar dream and the meaning may not be the same for each of them," Jenny responded.

Inwardly, intellectually although she knew this was true clinically, that she and Jeffrey shared almost the identical dream rattled her emotionally.

"Let's explore this further when we meet next week, shall we? Do you feel better now than when you came in today?" Jenny feigned a smile.

"Yes, Dr. Crawford. And I really hope I didn't offend you. I guess it was that transference you described. Thank you for understanding," Jeffrey added.

When Jeffrey left, Jenny scribbled a note in his file and then made a journal entry in her diary. She could hardly concentrate. The office phone rang. Her next appointment canceled. It gave her more time to ponder the strange connection between herself and Jeffrey. She had to sort out the confusion. Did her own attraction to him create the dream, or did some strange phenomenon occur here? The sexual nature of the dream did not disturb her half as much as the presence of the mysterious figure—and the curious "SS" symbol.

Jeffrey Clyman's apartment topped a mid-rise building overlooking the highway and the nearby warehouse district. The elevator creaked—when it worked at all, and the hallways smelled from the stray cats that wandered in and out. The fire escapes peeled with paint that covered the rust. Jeffrey convinced himself that living here he could save a little money and eventually, when he finished his law degree, move to a nicer neighborhood.

The sound of the school bus pulling up to the building woke him that morning, as it did nearly every morning. Slowly, he stretched and shook off his drowsiness. Dragging himself to the bathroom, he blinked his eyes and glanced in the dusty mirror. He nodded, as if to respond to the image looking back at him. At that moment, he felt older than his years. Perhaps the stress of his work at the law firm coupled with his rigorous class schedule and the intense studying had begun to take its toll on him. Or perhaps the loneliness of his solo lifestyle had finally etched itself on his person. Either way, Jeffrey plowed ahead with determination, vowing to earn that law degree. What price had he paid? His mother always told him, "Life is not a dress rehearsal; this is the performance." To date, he had no standing ovations and no curtain calls.

After a quick breakfast of buttered toast and coffee, Jeffrey bounded down the four flights of stairs, not willing to take the chance of getting stuck in the high-risk elevator. An old woman pushed her shopping cart past his front door, alternately mumbling to herself and looking up at the overcast sky. Her coat furled around her in the morning breeze. Oblivious to the leaves the wind flung past her, she plodded on. Jeffrey nearly bumped into her in his haste but paid her no mind. He checked his watch, then put the key in the car door, noticing that someone had scratched it with a sharp instrument. No surprise, considering the neighborhood. The old Buick cranked twice and then with a whine the engine roared.

Jeffrey entered the office building, briskly taking the marble steps two at a time. As he exited the elevator and swung the door to the office suite open, he came face to face with his boss, John Calendar. John Calendar had a reputation for ruthlessness among legal circles—and he had earned it. He barely nodded as Jeffrey walked past him to his desk. John Calendar cut an impressive figure, tall and imposing, impeccably dressed, with his slicked back salt and pepper gray hair and broad shoulders. He always sported mirrored glasses, even indoors. Jeffrey sensed something different about Mr. Calendar that day, but he couldn't put his finger on it at that moment. Instead, he focused his attention on the stack of folders and the pile of new papers on his desk. He carefully and meticulously reviewed every assignment the office manager had left him. Mr. Calendar always doled out the workload through the office manager, never directly to the firm's associates or to the legal assistants.

Just before lunch, the intercom on Jeffrey's desk phone rang. Uncharacteristically, Mr. Calendar himself called Jeffrey and summoned him to his office. Jeffrey felt himself tense up as he approached the spacious "inner sanctum", as the staff referred to it. The last time Jeffrey remembered entering Mr. Calendar's private office was the day he was hired and curtly welcomed aboard. He scanned the office, noticing the model ships and airplanes, the plaques and certificates lining the wall and the massive carved mahogany desk. Mr. Calendar stood with his back to Jeffrey, staring out the window. He at first spoke without even turning to face him.

"Clyman, I've been watching your work. I believe you show some promise. You're nearly done with your studies. You may have heard that James Chancellor will retire soon. That means we may have a place for you here as an associate. I trust that would interest you?" Mr. Calendar posed it as a question, turning to face Jeffrey.

Jeffrey, still standing, nodded silently—as if he did not believe what he had heard. Finally, Mr. Calendar motioned for him to take a seat. Jeffrey complied, waiting to hear what would follow. The two of them studied one another silently for a moment, like two wild animals sizing up their adversaries. Just then, Jeffrey noticed Mr. Calendar's rolled up sleeves. Instinctively—and he had no idea why, his eyes went to Mr. Calendar's forearm, where he saw that same marking as the man in the dream. The two intertwined "S's". Jeffrey's throat dried up. He adeptly looked away, to avoid arousing any suspicion.

Mr. Calendar settled into his high-backed chair, swiveled and continued.

"Of course the offer will hinge on your passing the bar exam successfully. That's all for now, Clyman."

"Th-thank you for your confidence in me, sir; I won't disappoint you," Jeffrey nearly stuttered as he rose from his chair.

That evening Jeffrey had no classes and no exams to prepare for. He had another important mission to accomplish. He drove home, changed his clothes, ate a quick dinner at the diner near his apartment building and headed back into the downtown district. Jeffrey pulled his car into the hospital parking lot. Avoiding the broken glass, he found a space at the far end of the lot and quickened his step. Stopping at the front desk, he procured a visitor's pass. They knew him by now. He had become a frequent visitor for the past year.

"Clyman, Room 432, Pulmonary Unit."

He took the dog-eared yellow index card from the same gray-haired volunteer with her hair in a bun that he saw every week. Nearly sliding out of the elevator, he passed the nurse's station. All around him he could hear the sounds of oxygen machines and respirators. He passed a tall Black orderly in a blue uniform, sloshing his mop across the gleaming tile floor. He slowed his pace as he approached the room. Two older men struggled to breathe, each hooked up to his own machines. A nurse with a clipboard briefly checked the machines, then left without acknowledging Jeffrey as he entered the room.

"Grandpa, it's me, Jeffrey. Don't try to talk; just listen, okay?"

Grandpa Clyman opened his eyes and forced a smile when he recognized Jeffrey. His condition had worsened since Jeffrey's last visit. The whites of his eyes appeared yellow, his skin sallow, his whole face seemed to sink. The oxygen mask had left a deep line. James Clyman had worked in the Pennsylvania coal mines for almost forty years until the company had extracted everything possible from the mine—and from its employees. Coal dust filled his lungs. The doctors had no cure. Nobody knew how much time he had left. Every breath proved an effort—if not an outright strain. It pained Jeffrey to see him like this, but he always came.

"Grandpa, I have good news for you. Today the Managing Partner of our law firm told me they had considered me for an upcoming associate's opening. I just have to finish my courses and pass the bar exam."

James Clyman took his grandson's hand and squeezed it. Even in his weakened state, he still had a good grip. Jeffrey knew it would give him some solace to hear good news. No one else came to visit him. Just then, a doctor came in. Jeffrey attempted to read the look on his face, but it revealed nothing. Jeffrey followed him into the hallway.

"Doctor, can you tell me anything at all?"

"We can only do our best to make him comfortable. I'm sorry, son."

The words stung, but they only reinforced what Jeffrey already knew intuitively. The end drew near for a good man. Jeffrey returned to the room, took the blanket from the chair and covered his grandfather. Leaning over, he kissed him on the forehead. His grandfather nodded his appreciation. Jeffrey departed.

As he slowly left the room and made his way down the hallway, the corridor seemed so much longer than it did on the way in to the room. Jeffrey passed a lone young man in a room by himself, sneaking a cigarette in the bathroom. No sooner did the curls of smoke peel out of the door than the young man began to wheeze and cough violently. Jeffrey debated with himself whether he should summon help. Just then, a nurse happened by and escorted the young man back to his bed.

The nurse, disgusted, passed Jeffrey as she stopped at the nurse's station, shaking her head and muttered, "Smoker—cancer's going to kill him for sure." Jeffrey thought about it as he descended in the elevator. Two people struggling to breathe—one because his job poisoned him; the other because he poisoned himself. He struggled to see the justice in it. Why did people throw away their lives?

The hulking older wing of the hospital loomed over Jeffrey's back as he walked to his car. He did not feel ready to let his grandfather go just yet. As he warmed up the car and backed out of the hospital parking lot, a sudden rush of memories gripped Jeffrey. He saw himself on the beach, in the park on the swing, on the amusement park carousel. His grandfather flashed by him in each scenario—always there for him. Then, like a television set changing from channel to channel, he flipped through a series of darker scenes in his mind. He couldn't stop it. From his father's violent death in a liquor store robbery to his cousin's long, horrible illness to his failed relationship with his ex-girlfriend, he began to feel out of control. It nearly panicked him as he pulled into the parking lot of his building. Exiting the car, the cool fall night air reinvigorated him. Jeffrey felt spent as he ascended the four flights of stairs to his apartment. He fumbled through his pockets until he found his keys. Opening the door, he looked around the living room, feeling like a stranger in his own home. He slumped down on the small couch and fell instantly into a deep sleep.

Across town, Jenny Crawford sat alone, recounting the hours of an uneventful day. She too fell into a deep sleep. Then the dreams came, one after another, like a series of home movies. Jenny lapsed back into her childhood memories. She watched herself open dolls at Christmas, ride her first bicycle and skate on the ice, effortlessly. Then, as if a reel fell off the projector, everything seemed to go dark.

Suddenly, bright light filled the room. Jenny stepped slowly through water that rose around her until she could no longer move. As the water rose to meet her mouth, she awoke, breathing heavily.

Jeffrey's dreams washed over him like waves of air. He replayed the same childhood scenes he recalled earlier that evening. Only it ended differently. Once again, he saw himself approaching Jenny Crawford, their arms outstretched to meet one another. He could feel the pace of his heartbeat quicken. Would she reject him at the last second?

Then he awoke to the sound of the neighbor's baby crying.

Jenny ambled her way into the tiny kitchen, focusing her eyes on the clock. Only midnight. The sound of a cat under her window caught her attention. It sounded so much like a human baby. She downed a glass of water and returned to the bedroom. This time she slept peacefully—until the last hour. The vision of the old man in the office building hallway crept back. He tried to speak to her this time. Had she internalized the account of Jeffrey's dream? Morning sent its cries to awake.

Jenny performed her usual morning ritual, showering, dressing, reading the newspaper and savoring that first cup of coffee. Nothing unusual. The dreams had dissipated; totally faded from consciousness. The Mustang roared as she fired up the engine. Traffic sang to her. She glanced at the radio dial; then she decided to ignore it. The brisk morning air had frosted her office windows. No matter. Jenny opened the office door, switched on the lights and swung around, half expecting to see the old man's shadowy figure. No one. She resumed preparing for her day's patients, poring over files and her journal entries. She recognized the gentle knock on the outer door as Jeffrey entered.

Jeffrey sank into the couch, appearing piqued. His usual energy lacking, he let his head slip between his hands, gently rubbing his temples. Jenny came out from behind her desk and approached him, showing concern. She drew a chair up to him, placing her hand on his head. Jeffrey slowly raised his head, feeling the warmth of her hand. He began shaking his head as his eyes teared up. Jenny reached out her arms and wrapped them around his shoulders, gently rocking back and forth with him. Finally, he spoke.

"Dr. Crawford; may I call you Jenny? I can't seem to focus on my work or my studies. It's more than I can handle. I don't think it's the job pressures. The dreams keep haunting me; and those people with the "SS" marking on their arms—I've seen more of them. What is happening to me?"

Jenny backed slowly away, re-establishing her composure and wearing her professional mask. It didn't last. It began to crack. She let out a long sigh, then leaned in to Jeffrey.

"Jeffrey, it's not you. I don't know who or what they are, but they are here and for some strange reason; they are trying to speak to us. I have had the dreams as well. Speaking as both your therapist and as your friend, I want you to start keeping a journal. Write down every dream and every sighting. We will compare notes and we will figure this out, I promise you."

Jenny nodded. Jeffrey echoed her gesture and felt relief. They concluded the session with a longer than usual gaze into each other's eyes. Jeffrey quickly departed the office, still somewhat upset but calmer and less stressed than when he arrived. As he closed the door, he darted one quick glance back to see if Jenny was watching. Scanning the dark hallway, he did a double take. Had his eyes played a trick on him? On the wall, he thought he saw the words "They are here" scrawled. He did not look back, but instead, bounded down the steps and ran to his car.

Jeffrey resolved to plow through his workload and his studies without incident. The week seemed to dissolve in a flurry of meetings, books, papers and research. He still felt nervous when he passed Mr. Calendar in the hallway, his sleeves rolled up revealing that "SS" marking on his forearm. He couldn't avoid him. Now, the powerful lead attorney acknowledged Jeffrey with direct eye contact and a feigned smile when he breezed by him. Ever since that brief cursory meeting in Mr. Calendar's office, Jeffrey felt watched—almost stalked, like prey. Finally, Friday rolled around, and Jeffrey felt a sense of relief. He began stuffing a few carefully selected case files into his briefcase when he noticed Mr. Calendar staring in his direction from across the room. Jeffrey continued, switched off his desk lamp and left the building, still uneasy.

After a quick stop home, Jeffrey changed his clothes, stopped at the diner and sat at the counter alone. After ordering, he recognized the man sitting next to him. A well-known local figure, the County Sheriff smiled at him over his cup of coffee. Jeffrey knew him by name and reputation, but not personally. His boss knew him well. They had spent many moments together in the halls of the courthouse. Jeffrey tried not to look obvious, but it had become his habit of late to discreetly check everyone's arms for "the mark" as he had come to know it. Long sleeves covered the sheriff's arms. No way to tell. Jeffrey imagined himself spilling water on the man in an effort to get him to reveal his arm. He did not have the nerve to do it. He would just have to wait to find out, he reasoned. He wondered to himself which emotion would win out eventually—fear or anger. He still had no reason for anger. What had these people done to him, after all? He pondered the question, gazing at the man's reflection in the glass doors of the diner's dessert case. No reason. Just emotion. They can't co-exist. One has to win out. Just then the sheriff leaned over and spoke to him.

"You work for John Calendar, don't you? I've seen you at the courthouse."

Jeffrey nodded, waved his arms to get the waitress's attention, grabbed his check and promptly left. He didn't look back but felt the sheriff's eyes on his back.

As he did every week, Jeffrey sat in the last of the rush hour traffic as he made his way to the hospital. He nervously fiddled with the radio dial, flipping from station to station. He sought distraction, trying to find some solace in the news of the larger world around him. Each newscast carried the same top of the hour lead story—more deaths in Viet Nam. Secretly, Jeffrey felt relieved that he didn't have to shoulder a gun. It clashed with his character. In his heart, he simply did not understand war. What drove people to think they had the right to kill other people? He snapped the knob on the car radio so hard it nearly fell off. He hadn't even realized the extent of his pent-up anger.

Pulling in to the hospital lot, he slammed the car door and proceeded at a brisk pace toward the building. A light rain began first as a drizzle, then punctuated the cool evening. Wiping the droplets off of his jacket, Jeffrey met the smiling receptionist, took his guest pass and quickened his pace toward the elevator. When he entered his grandfather's room, something seemed different. He scanned the room, noticing the other bed, now empty, but with personal objects strewn about, as if someone else had been there and just left. His grandfather slept, the oxygen machines breathing loudly, its rhythm like a drumbeat. As usual, if he arrived and found his grandfather asleep, Jeffrey pulled up a chair near the foot of the bed and waited.

A half hour must have passed; Jeffrey began to doze off, then awoke with a start as a nurse entered the room. He did not recognize her. She checked each of the machines that Mr. Clyman had connected to him, nodded reassuringly to Jeffrey and left without speaking. No sooner than she left, a doctor entered. Jeffrey had never seen this doctor before. Gray haired with a mustache, the man had a swarthy complexion. Short in stature and very deliberate in gait, he eyed Jeffrey, then spoke.

"You are the grandson, yes?"

He spoke with an accent. Jeffrey couldn't quite place the man's country of origin. Jeffrey nodded.

"Please. Step out for a few moments. Go to the visitor's lounge at the end of the hall while I perform the exam."

Jeffrey reluctantly arose from the chair as the doctor drew the curtain around his grandfather's bed. Jeffrey suspiciously eyed the doctor as he slowly began to depart the room. Jeffrey was well acquainted with the lounge at the end of the hall. Old, wrinkled magazines populated the tables and the acrid smell of stale smoke hung in the air. He didn't want to spend a moment there. Instead, he began to nervously pace up and down the hallway. Jeffrey glanced in at the young smoker across the hall. The thought occurred to him that this person had thrown his life away while his grandfather clung to life.

Just then, something caught Jeffrey's attention. At first, he thought he imagined it. A low whirring sound unlike anything he had ever heard emanated from his grandfather's room. He approached the room cautiously, peeking in. The curtain still drawn, Jeffrey could see the doctor's silhouette as he hovered over the elder Mr. Clyman. Suddenly, a mysterious blue light enveloped the bed. At that exact moment, Jeffrey heard an agonizing scream from across the hall. As he poked his head out, he heard the young man gasping for breath.

Then, only the pounding rhythm of the oxygen machine continued. A nurse rushed into the young man's room. In a panic, she ran to the nurse's station and grabbed the intercom, summoning a doctor.

"Room 424, Code Blue."

A commotion began as a doctor, the nurse and an aide rushed into the room. Too late. Dead quiet. Jeffrey turned his attention back to his grandfather's room. The whirring sound had stopped. The blue light had disappeared—and so had the doctor. Jeffrey thought he had imagined the whole incident—until he re-entered the room. His grandfather sat up and smiled at him. A healthy glow had returned to his once sallow complexion. Jeffrey still could not believe what he saw. Eyes wide, he approached his grandfather.

"Grandpa, how do you feel?" he struggled to get the words out.

"Never better, Jeffrey; never better. It's good to see you."

Jeffrey stared at him in disbelief.

"I'll be right back, grandpa."

Jeffrey ran to the nurse's station and begged the nurse to find his grandfather's doctor. Moments later, Jeffrey and the pulmonary specialist entered the room, observing a cheerful patient reading a magazine.

"Mr. Clyman, your grandson tells me you are feeling better. Let's have a look."

Doctor Hirsch removed the oxygen mask from Mr. Clyman, placing his stethoscope on his chest. He then checked his watch as he held the older man's wrist, taking his pulse. A confused smile crept over his face.

"I can't explain it, but it's as if somehow you miraculously recovered. Your breathing seems stronger, your pulse is normal. I'm going to keep you here for a couple of days of observation. We're not going to continue with the oxygen. Let's see how you do."

Doctor Hirsch nodded and smiled to Mr. Clyman and motioned for Jeffrey to accompany him out into the hallway.

"In over twenty-five years of practice, I've never seen anything like this. Tomorrow, I'm going to order new X-rays and see if we can make any sense of this. I don't want you to delude yourself. You call me or come by tomorrow night when we have the results. I'll tell you when we have something more conclusive."

Jeffrey watched Doctor Hirsch as he turned the corner of the hallway. Then, the scene across the hall caught his attention. The team of doctor, nurse and aid silently left the room across the hall. Jeffrey peered in after they departed. An orderly steered the bed toward the doorway. Jeffrey watched as he covered the lifeless young man's body with a sheet and slowly removed him from the room. Jeffrey imagined them taking him down to the hospital morgue—a place he never wanted to see. With that, Jeffrey turned his attention back to his grandfather.

For the first time he could remember, Jeffrey watched with delight as his grandfather actually devoured a meal with gusto. After finishing, the elder Mr. Clyman pushed back the tray and smiled.

"Not bad for hospital food; not bad at all."

Both men laughed. Jeffrey stood up, leaning over his grandfather.

"I'm thrilled to see you feeling this well. I'll be back tomorrow night. You sleep well."

Jeffrey hugged his grandfather and quickly left the room, dashing down the hallway. Mixed emotions gripped him. The excitement, the awe and the fear fought inside of him. The elevator door opened; he jumped in, nearly bumping in to an orderly with a supply cart. Returning the guest pass to the receptionist, Jeffrey literally ran to his car. The rain had come down harder, waxing the surface of the parking lot. Large drops danced across his windshield. Jeffrey peeled out of the parking lot, skidding on the wet leaves and heading home.

Parking the car behind the building, Jeffrey climbed the stairs with a fury. As soon as he entered the apartment, he ran for the telephone. Feverishly dialing and out of breath, he left a hurried message on the answering machine.

"Jenny—uh, Doctor Crawford, this is Jeffrey Clyman. Please call me as soon as you get this message. I need to speak with you right away. It's about 9 PM. If you happen to get this tonight, please call me at home. Thank you."

Jeffrey collapsed into a chair, his heart pounding. Every sound resonated in his ears. Passing cars. Neighbor's cats. Crying babies. Ticking clocks. Even the buzz of the refrigerator. He kept replaying the scenes in his head. He still could not accept what his eyes and ears had witnessed. One man dies; another man regains life, at exactly the same moment. Divine or demonic? Does it matter? How could this happen?

As Jeffrey sat nervously waiting for the phone to ring, across town at St. Elizabeth's, the other hospital, a similar scene followed. A drug addict in the alley way rolled over and died at exactly the same moment as a patient upstairs stood up and walked for the first time in weeks, as the blue light faded. No witnesses. No crime. Just a miracle.

Jeffrey nervously paced the floor of the living room in his apartment, scuffing the area rug. He began muttering to himself, trying to make sense of what he had seen and heard. He waited; he stared at the telephone. It refused to ring. His anxiety level rose. His heart pounding in his ears, he caved into a chair. A solitary light bulb burned in the overhead. He could practically hear his own breathing. Finally, he could not sit still anymore. He knew if he didn't go out, the dry steam heat from the radiators would put him to sleep. He did not want to succumb to sleep. By 10 PM, he decided Jenny would not get the message and call him before morning. He grabbed his jacket, ran for the elevator and dashed out into the heavy rain. A few random passersby huddled under umbrellas past his building. Jeffrey threw the car door open. The interior became soaked before he could even close the door. With a whine and a crack, the engine roared.

The windshield wipers whipped across the window. The scene blurred as the haze of streetlights flashed across the intersection. As the traffic light turned red, Jeffrey punched the buttons on the car radio. An ambulance whizzed by, siren blaring and lights flashing furiously. Jeffrey froze as the static stopped and he heard the newscaster interrupt the program.

"We now bring you a special report, live from the newsroom. A curious series of hospital deaths occurred across the tri-state area this evening. They remain unexplained, according to several hospital spokespersons. We were unable to speak to any of the doctors involved, but an anonymous source has sent a cryptic message to our news desk. We will continue to update you on this story as we learn more."

Jeffrey nearly collided with an oncoming truck as the light turned green and he left the intersection. He made a radical decision. Pulling up to the drug store on Broad Street, he ran into the telephone booth. He had always respected Dr. Crawford's privacy, but this demanded her attention. He thumbed through the tattered phone book, found her number and dialed it. It rang incessantly. Where could she be at this hour, he thought? Just as he nearly let the receiver drop, he heard her familiar voice.

"Jenny, ah, Dr. Crawford, it's Jeffrey Clyman. I need to see you right now. No, not on the phone. Where can I meet you? The diner, on Morris Avenue? Come quickly, please."

Out of breath, Jeffrey hung up the phone and darted back into the car. He turned the heater up in an effort to dry himself off. He so desperately needed Jenny to believe him. He knew he needed to *look* credible, too. He made his way around the side streets through the flooding as the rain began to subside. The bright lights of the diner greeted him. He pulled into an empty space close to the door. Jenny's Mustang eased into the space beside him. He wished he had an umbrella at that moment. Jenny pulled her raincoat around her, and they ran for the door together. Only a few patrons; good, Jeffrey thought—we'll have more privacy. They took the last booth in the back, ordered coffee and Jeffrey took Jenny's hands in his own. He felt her warmth—and her sincerity as he made direct eye contact with her.

"You are going to think I have totally lost my sanity when you hear what I am about to tell you," Jeffrey blurted out, carefully keeping his voice low.

"Go ahead. Let me be the judge of that," Jenny tried to lighten his mood.

Jeffrey related the details of what he had witnessed when he visited his grandfather at the hospital...and the newscast he heard on the car radio. He paused, waiting for her judgment. No judgment. Jenny's eyes widened. She sat back, sipping her coffee. Lowering her cup, she raised her eyes to meet his and spoke.

"You are sure you didn't fall asleep at the hospital? No chance that you dreamt any of this?" she confronted him, not accusing, but genuinely probing.

"I tell you I haven't slept since early this morning. Not a moment. When I got home, my adrenaline kept me awake. I know it sounds too weird, but you have to believe me. This is real. Do you think this is connected to the people with the "SS" mark?

Jenny paused, taking it in and considering everything Jeffrey recounted before rendering an opinion. She reached across the table, placing her hand on top of his trembling hand.

"Yes, I believe you and yes, I do think there is a connection. I just don't know any more than you do about this—or where to begin to try and figure it out. I think we just have to watch and see what unfolds. We don't know who they are, where they came from, what they want or whether they mean us any harm. We just have to stay in close contact and keep each other informed, " Jenny did her best to soothe his anxiety.

They both nodded in agreement and arose from the booth, heading for the cashier. As they began to leave, Jeffrey instinctively turned around. He caught a glimpse of a man approaching and instantly recognized him as the Sheriff. He hustled Jenny out into the rain, which had lightened up to a steady drizzle.

"I know that man. He may be one of them, but I can't be sure. I haven't seen the mark, but he knows my boss and John Calendar is definitely one of *them.* Come on. Let's go."

Jeffrey led Jenny to her car, leaned over and gently kissed her forehead.

"Thank you, thank you. I don't know what I would have done if you didn't come."

They each drove off into the night, in opposite directions.

That weekend, after his regular Saturday morning errands, Jeffrey had to play in the firm's soccer game. They used the high school field to square off against a rival law firm in town. The firm required participation from all of its able-bodied partners and associates—but generally not from its support staff. They simply had to attend and cheer the team on. When Frank Stanton broke his arm, John Calendar himself asked Jeffrey to suit up and play. The game moved quickly. It gave Jeffrey an opportunity to engage with other more senior players in the firm—people he seldom interacted with. It also gave him a vantage point to observe them as people. He watched every move John Calendar made. As ruthless on the field as in the courtroom, he did not disappoint anyone. He always played to win. It was never "just a game" to him. Jeffrey watched him score again and again. His opponents seemed to tire as he gained his momentum. Jeffrey wondered about that. Did the "marked" men have some secret energy source that replenished their strength? He would just have to wait to find out.

"Not bad, Clyman; you had a few good plays there. Maybe we should make you a regular on this team," John Calendar asserted to Jeffrey. Still, his every move seemed so calculated. Even the way he waited for a response.

"I'd like that, sir. I wouldn't disappoint you," Jeffrey confided.

The game tired Jeffrey out. He decided to stay home and rest, putting his studies aside and declining his friends' urging to go out for the evening.

Ten miles away in the affluent suburb of Westfield, later that afternoon John Calendar placed a series of phone calls, each with the identical message.

"Yes, the poker game is tonight at 8 PM at the usual place. Don't be late. I expect all of the players."

The wrought iron gates opened, allowing each of the cars in the procession to enter the Calendar estate. The gates bore the initials "JC". The ground still wet from the recent deluge, each of the long black limousines pulled up the long semi-circular driveway to the steps of the large white Georgian mansion. The door swung open, and the butler took each man's coat, ushering them all into the dining room. A fire blazed in the fireplace, illuminating the figure of John Calendar. He turned to greet the men as they took their usual places at the long marble table.

"Senator Reichstag; Congressman Foley; Assemblyman Foresythe; Governor Hutchinson; and Doctors Mustafa and Steinman. Shall we get started?"

The question was rhetorical—more of an order than an inquiry. John Calendar scanned the room and its occupants like an X-ray machine.

"Our plan has been set into motion. We each have a role to play. Our orders are to continue seeking out and switching the souls of the unworthy who throw away their lives with those deserving to live and have been deprived of living a healthy life. We need to accomplish this as quickly and as quietly as we can while drawing as little attention to ourselves and our mission as possible."

They all nodded their heads silently. In characteristic fashion, John Calendar waited for responses from the group. Governor Hutchinson arose from his seat.

"What mechanisms do we have in place to assure us that no one witnesses our activity?"

Remaining in control, John Calendar deferred the question to the appropriate team member.

"Senator Reichstag, would you like to speak to the Governor's concern?"

"Certainly. We have no mechanism to prevent anyone from witnessing our activity. We do, however, have the facility to ensure that we can control any witnesses."

Congressman Foley echoed his colleague's response.

"I assure you nobody will take them seriously. We control the funding for the hospitals—and that includes the mental institutions. We can admit them quietly, without incident."

John Calendar appeared satisfied, addressing the group.

"Any other concerns anyone would like to express?"

Governor Hutchinson slowly stood up again, placing his hands on the table and gestured.

"What about the press? I've already heard they have reported incidents. How do we control them? I'm not sure we can."

John Calendar strode across the room, motioning to Governor Hutchinson to resume taking his seat.

"Every one and every thing *can* and *will* be controlled. I will illustrate. Have you been following the headlines about the AIDS outbreak? An unfortunate situation, to be sure. An earlier experiment gone bad, to be candid. We thought we could control the outbreak and keep it contained. But humans will be humans. Social creatures share everything. Yes, we created it in a laboratory. Now that the genie is out of the bottle, we simply plant stories to deflect attention away from the real cause. We call it 'disinformation.' Rest assured, it works."

With that statement concluded, the butler returned with a tray full of brandy glasses, a decanter of liquor and a box of cigars. The fire roared. The men drank and smoked. The night sky darkened even more.

The very next night a massive power failure blanketed the region. Radio and television transmissions were knocked out. Streetlights and traffic lights faded one by one. Some speculated that a storm coming in from the mid-West took out the power. Power company officials had no answers—or did they? Under cover of darkness, a series of deaths occurred at area hospitals. They appeared to be random, but were they? Perhaps the machines we had come to rely on to keep our loved ones alive had failed in the wake of the power outage. Perhaps not. Only a small group of people knew the truth. Doctors and nurses scurried about with flashlights, to no avail. That night, some seventy people died in hospitals around the region. Who died, and why? The medical examiners would have a long day ahead of them. Days later, as each medical examiner completed his work, he searched for answers, for some pattern—to no avail. Strangely, each person appeared to have died at precisely the same moment, yet each from a different cause. When the power came back on, the hospital staffs noted that most of the patients survived the outage. During the confusion, no one noticed the blue light emanating from a few selected rooms, accompanied by a low buzzing hum.

Newspaper and radio station reporters carried stories of the mysterious power outage—and the story ended there. Like a thief in the night, someone stole the lives of the undeserving...quietly, without fanfare. Dogs barked; babies cried; and life went on.

Jeffrey Clyman had slept through most of the blackout—rest he needed vitally. Jenny Crawford had taken one of her few trips out of town that weekend to visit family, returning with no knowledge of what had occurred in her absence. Only the stopped clocks gave a hint that anything at all had happened...and that in and of itself simply did not arouse her suspicion. Jeffrey, however, did pick up on the next day's headlines—and they troubled him. He even began to clip and assemble the articles in the journal Jenny had told him to keep. He began to brood, flipping the pages and tracing the recent events. He had no idea how close he stood to one of the most powerful of these people. He began to call them the "Soul Switchers" in his journal. He became more and more anxious as he tried to connect the dots and make sense of it all. He awaited his next session with Dr. Crawford, hoping she could help him. He began to question his sanity.

In the middle of the week, Jeffrey found himself once again overwhelmed with the firm's legal work and with his law studies. All the better, he thought, to take his mind off of the strange occurrences that plagued him. While poring over case files, he suddenly looked up. As he did, he noticed John Calendar seemingly staring his way. Then, the intercom on his desk phone buzzed. Mr. Calendar again uncharacteristically summoned him to his office personally. Jeffrey entered with that same uneasiness as in the past, even though outwardly he had no reason for it.

"Have a seat, Clyman. Cigar? Oh, I forgot; you don't smoke."

Mr. Calendar stopped leaning over his desk and descended into his high-backed chair.

"Ever go hunting, Clyman?"

"Uh, no sir. I never did," Jeffrey replied sheepishly.

"This weekend, I want you to join our little hunting party. Just come. I'll have Janelle the receptionist give you directions to the cabin. Be on time."

When John Calendar said, "I want you to...", it meant you had to do it. Jeffrey certainly had no interest in hunting, but nonetheless, if it pleased the boss, he would go.

Jeffrey's grandfather had returned home after his recovery. While the rest of the family hailed it as a miracle, in spite of his happiness, it troubled Jeffrey. He had difficulty sleeping again. He resisted the temptation to use any sleep aids. When he finally fell asleep, the dreams came again. Jeffrey saw himself surrounded by the marked men, in the center of a circle. They didn't say anything; they just stared blankly at him, then faded away. He turned and ran, coming face to face with them again. They surrounded him again. Then he heard the whirring sound and the blue light covered everything. In a moment, the noise stopped; the light faded; they disappeared. Jeffrey awoke, his mouth parched and his palms sweating. He had never experienced physical symptoms from a dream before. He began to wonder if he really had dreamt it. Finally, he fell back to sleep. He dreamt that Jenny Crawford came to him this time. He welcomed her in to his bed. As soon as he reached over to touch her, she faded away. Darkness.

The crisp Saturday morning air filled Jeffrey's lungs as he belted down a cup of coffee while warming up the engine of his car. He defrosted the windows slowly, peering out as the early morning sun began to pierce the sky above. Jeffrey followed the directions Janelle had given him, arriving at the cabin. A few of the firm's associates stood on the porch, along with a couple of other men Jeffrey did not recognize. They all seemed to stare him down as he sheepishly exited the car and approached them. They nodded but continued their conversation. Jeffrey felt like an outsider. The door to the cabin opened and John Calendar strode out, surveying the group.

"I've asked young Mr. Clyman here to join us on his first ever hunting trip," the phrasing seemed so pejorative.

"Please show him every courtesy. Grab your gear; let's go," John Calendar barked the words like a drill sergeant giving orders.

The party began its trek into the woods. As they approached a clearing, each man took his place and began to position his weapon. John Calendar motioned to Jeffrey to follow him into the blind—a tiny hut covered with leaves to serve as camouflage. He placed his finger on his lips, indicating silence. Then he motioned outside, and Jeffrey noticed a deer approaching. The buck moved cautiously toward the blind, then stopped and held its position. Jeffrey noticed both the majesty and the serenity of the creature. So swift and yet so helpless, he thought. It ended in an instant. The crack of a rifle from a member of the party and the buck fell, helpless. Its legs quivered as blood gushed out of its chest. Its eyes stared directly at Jeffrey. He cupped his hand over his mouth and darted out of the blind, vomiting profusely on the forest floor behind the blind.

When he finally had the strength to look up, John Calendar stood over him. Jeffrey felt the color return to his face in embarrassment.

"I'm sorry, sir. If this was a test, I guess I failed miserably."

"Actually, not. You passed with flying colors. You place a high value on life."

Jeffrey's confusion must have shown. He shook his head in disbelief. Not at all what he expected. As he surveyed the departing hunting party, he noticed one man missing from the group. Jeffrey instinctively turned back towards the woods in time to hear that haunting, now familiar whirring sound followed by a blue light. He started toward the group. The missing member emerged from the edge of the woods. Jeffrey heard a faint rustling, then caught a glimpse of a deer as it disappeared into the forest.

Monday morning Jeffrey awoke to his usual ritual, dashing out the door to work. As he stepped out of the elevator and into the law office suite, he reached under his coat and presented Janelle the receptionist with a cup of coffee. The surprised look on her face caught him off guard. Such a small gesture of kindness seldom elicited a dramatic reaction. Before he could leave, she took his arm and pulled him towards her.

"It's just a cup of coffee; I thought you should have one, too," Jeffrey smiled at her.

"You have no idea what it's like to be a colored woman working in a White man's law firm. Thank you so much. That is the nicest thing anyone has done since I've been here."

Jeffrey could hardly believe what he had heard. After all, a hundred years had passed since slavery ended. He proceeded to his desk and began sorting through the pile of case files, setting them in priority order. He had a long day ahead of him. At the end of the day, he switched off his desk lamp, picked up his briefcase and headed for the door. Nearly everyone had left for the night. With most of the lights off, the office looked like a ghost ship. As he exited, he heard a gasp. Turning around, he saw Frank Stanton with his hands on Janelle. She didn't move. Jeffrey waited in the hallway for the elevator, half curious and half concerned. Janelle broke away from Frank, grabbed her coat and stood by Jeffrey's side. They waited silently.

Jeffrey's curiosity got the better of him. He started his car, began defrosting the windows and pretended to clear off the leaves that had populated it. Janelle briskly walked around the corner, looking over her shoulder from time to time. Jeffrey turned off the engine. He saw a figure striding at a quick pace. He decided to follow, out of concern. It looked like Frank. Jeffrey hung back but kept up with both of them. Suddenly, he saw Frank come up behind Janelle, cup his hand over her mouth and maneuver her into an alley way. Jeffrey stayed in the shadows, coming closer. Now he could hear her every breath.

"You only give it to guys that *pay* you, is that it?"

"Stay away from me or I'll have my brother break your other arm."

"He won't even clean toilets in your bastard son's school when I'm done."

With one swift kick, Janelle brought Frank down. Jeffrey breathed a sigh of relief and headed back to his car. Not that much had changed in a hundred years.

Jeffrey vacillated between a state of anxiety and one of calm over the soul switchers, as he had come to call them. He still could not figure out who they were, where they came from and what motivated them. Moreover, he could hardly discern their overall game plan. His edginess continued, as his quest to discover more about them got the better of him. He tempered it with caution, however. More and more, his therapy sessions focused on the soul switchers. Finally, he confessed to Jenny:

"I'm trying not to obsess over this, but we have to know more about these people. We just have to find out what they are up to."

"Jeffrey, you said, '*we* have to know'. Are you aware of what you said?" Jenny gave him her best clinical stare.

"Well, it's no longer about me. It's about everyone. You've got to help me, Dr. Crawford."

"Jeffrey, I am helping you. I'm helping you deal with your feelings and your attitudes—with the way you deal with the circumstances in your life. It's all about the choices you make and how you *react* to what happens," Jenny counseled him.

"No, I mean I need you to help me find out what these people are doing. Maybe you need to see them in action for yourself, Dr. Crawford."

Jenny felt the lure of his obsession pulling at her. She resisted it. Then he recounted the story of the hunting party, and his resulting confusion.

"You saw that man here in your office building a few months ago. You know I'm not making any of this up," Jeffrey pleaded.

"I never implied that you did. But you need to get on with your life. By your own admission, you have more important things to attend to. You need to pass that bar exam," she offered.

"Just once, if you would witness one of these occurrences for yourself, you might change your mind," Jeffrey implored her.

"Jeffrey, it's not like we have a schedule of when and where they will occur, and can show up to observe them," she appealed to his sensible side.

"What if I could photograph or film one? Do you think anyone would believe me?" Jeffrey countered.

"Jeffrey...stop and listen to yourself. We don't know that they have any nefarious plans. Let it go. Stay vigilant; keep your eyes and ears open; keep the journal, but stay focused on your own personal goals," Jenny reached across the desk, placed her hand on his and looked right into his eyes.

The rest of 1966 came and went in a blur. Jeffrey's grandfather passed away quietly of natural causes; Jeffrey passed the bar exam and became an associate in the firm; he redirected his efforts toward his career and the soul switchers covertly continued their work.

Chapter II

1976

Ten years passed since Jeffrey became an associate in John Calendar's firm. Mr. Calendar set him up under the watchful eye of one of his senior associates, who tirelessly mentored Jeffrey. Jeffrey became a skilled litigator. The experience helped him overcome his over cautiousness, yet he retained his kind and thoughtful nature. He became somewhat of a paradox—assertive, yet not aggressive; confident, but never displaying bravado. He had learned through observation to control the controllable things. The practice of law taught him how to choose his battles wisely. As hard as he needed to work for the firm, he began to build more of a life for himself. His mother had passed away, but her words remained with him. "Life is not a dress rehearsal." He began to act in a local community theater group. He craved and had finally found an outlet for self-expression.

The winter thaw had finally arrived. After a harsh January and February of biting winds and low temperatures, the first hint of spring nearing came with a few warm late March days. The hard ground finally gave way to a gradual softening; a hint of blue returned to the skies, and Jeffrey could feel the warmth of the sun on his face. He stayed in the same apartment, despite his increased income, but relented and finally bought a new car. As he started the engine, the radio came on with a newscaster rambling on about the current economic woes. Another recession had taken hold of America, with President Gerald Ford pledging to pull us through it. He began by making an example of government workers, holding their pay at current levels. It would literally take an act of Congress for them to get a raise.

Jeffrey had taken to rewarding himself for the week's hard work with Saturday morning breakfast at the diner. The hostess greeted him.

Before she could lead him to a table, he brushed past her and stood over the familiar figure. Jenny looked up from her coffee with a start.

"Mind if I join you, doctor?" he queried with a smile.

"Not at all; please do, counselor."

They both laughed. The years had not changed her much. They both appeared more self-assured. And they both sensed the strong connection that time could never erase. Jeffrey reached across the table and took both of her hands in his. Drawing them up to his lips, he kissed them gently.

"I'm not your patient anymore; just a friend who greatly admires you and always cared about you," Jeffrey confided in her.

"And I'm not the twenty-six-year-old virgin you knew either," Jenny retorted, tossing her head back and laughing.

"Then I guess we should make it official and call this our first date," Jeffrey replied.

"No, that would be tonight," Jenny slid her hand over his.

"To tonight, then," Jeffrey raised his coffee cup.

Their dinner date went well, as they both caught up on the last ten years of one another's lives. The long stares, the repressed emotions seemed to melt into a love connection. At the same time, ten miles away, the Calendar estate buzzed with activity. Important guests arrived; another session got under way.

As always, judges, Congressman, Senators, prominent lawyers and doctors assembled in the great room. The fire blazed; the high and mighty marked men raised their concerns; and their movement gained momentum.

"We had an incident early in the game, sir. One of our operatives had gone rogue, if you recall. And we believe he may have exposed us to someone," the Senator offered.

John Calendar arose from his seat at the head of the table—referred to by the others as "the throne". He leaned forward, placing both hands on the table as he responded.

"And we sent him back. Let Command deal with him. Nothing happened then and we have no reason to believe anything will happen now."

"The current political climate favors our mission. We have quelled the radical unrest; people feel more secure with a stronger military presence at home. The public doesn't like change," a congressman attempted to assuage any fears.

"Still, there is the matter of the press. They still find out information and they are not afraid to expose it," the newly elected governor chimed in.

"Then we need to penetrate that community, quickly and quietly," John Calendar pounded the table with his fist, emphatically.

The group agreed and began to formulate its plan to infiltrate the ranks of the newspaper, radio and television stations. As the cognac and cigars made their way around the room, ten miles away, things began to move at a rapid pace.

Leaving the restaurant, Jeffrey settled Jenny into his car and looked her directly in the eye.

"Your place or mine?"

"Much to his surprise, Jenny leaned over and whispered in his ear.

"Yours. Definitely yours—and step on it."

The Sunday morning sun crashed through Jeffrey's apartment window. He awoke with a start, questioning whether last night actually happened or whether he dreamt it. The sound of eggs frying and the smell of coffee wafting in to his bedroom gave him his answer. He lumbered in to the kitchen to see Jenny putting the finishing touches on a breakfast fit for a king. He studied her. He could hardly believe she had spent the night with him. He secretly feared she would slip away. He came up behind her, placed his arms on her waist, leaned over and turned her to face him. The long kiss felt like it would never end.

"Did you have pleasant dreams?" she asked, pouring his coffee.

"Ever the therapist. Yes, I did; whatever I remember of them. I think we got married."

She tossed a piece of toast at his plate playfully.

"Hmm. Mrs. Jeffrey Clyman. That's not exactly a nightmare."

"And what did *you* dream about?" Jeffrey drained the cup of coffee.

"Not quite as pleasant as yours. I dreamt your soul switchers plotted and took over every branch of government." She said it deadpan.

"Seriously?" he took her hand.

"Seriously," she nodded.

He dismissed the dream.

"What would you like to do today?" he asked.

"What we did last night," she answered, pulling him out of his chair.

John Calendar's home phone seldom rang on a Sunday morning. He had given the help the day off and answered it himself.

"To what do I owe the honor, Mr. Secretary?" he half growled, knowing it had to have serious overtones.

"Have you heard the National Weather Service's reports of high volatility sunspot activity yet?" the Secretary sounded gravely concerned.

"Yes. Go on," John Calendar waited impatiently for the reply.

"Well, it's causing tears in the space-time continuum, according to our sources at NASA. We have tremendous swirls around the triangle. This could prove very disruptive to our personnel as they move into place," the Secretary of State continued.

"Then we will stay put and hope it doesn't send anybody back. Suspend all travel and keep us informed, please. We can't afford to lose any of our operatives in transit."

John Calendar hung up the phone, turned in his chair and surveyed the sky around him. To others, it was just the sky. To him, it could prove disastrous to their plans. He wondered just how far it could set them back if the sunspot activity continued. They had never experienced this before. Evidently nature still held sway over what even the most powerful people could control.

As the weeks passed, Jenny and Jeffrey spent more time together. Their relationship just seemed to fall into place naturally. Still, neither one of them wanted to push the other. They let things happen at their own pace. Both of them, however, secretly feared the other might one day decide to leave. Perhaps the fear of abandonment becomes ingrained at an early age—especially when one loses a loved one. Jenny and Jeffrey both kept their relationship quiet, choosing not to share the news with their families. After several months of sharing their weekends, Jeffrey felt the time had come to make a commitment. Jenny sensed it, too, welcoming it.

"I think one of us should give up an apartment," he announced.

"Okay", Jenny replied, facing him across the kitchen table.

"Which one?" she queried playfully.

"The one with the higher rent, of course," Jeffrey responded.

"You just don't like my pink drapes and bedspread," she teased.

"Done. We'll bring all your pink stuff over here. Just don't tell anyone I work with," he retorted.

Moving in together felt right to both of them. They saved some money and managed to spend more time together. They both cherished their weekends. Each had a relaxing effect on the other. Sunday rolled around. Jeffrey returned from the firm's basketball game, dropped his gym bag down and strolled into the bedroom. Jenny sat on the bed. He sensed something bothering her.

"Did you burn my dinner? What could be so overwhelming that my former therapist has that look on her face?"

"I'm pregnant," Jenny blurted out.

Jeffrey stopped in his tracks and stared at her.

"You don't seem too pleased yourself," Jenny choked back tears.

"Wrong again, future Mrs. Clyman," Jeffrey cupped her face in his hands and kissed her as the tears streamed down her cheeks.

"I guess I will sleep okay tonight, after all," Jenny breathed a sigh of relief.

Suddenly, the well-kept secret became a cause for celebration as Jenny and Jeffrey began to make their wedding plans. The couple made their own wedding, keeping it simple and inviting just the closest friends and co-workers. The honeymoon would have to wait. Jeffrey gave up his theater group in order to spend more time with Jenny and closely monitor her pregnancy. Jenny cut back her patient schedule, first to four, then three days a week as the pregnancy progressed. The doctor visits became more frequent as time went on and morning sickness kicked in. Jeffrey could not break away when he had a trial but managed to take Jenny whenever he could.

The phone on Jeffrey's desk rang—and rang—and rang. He returned from the men's room just in time to grab it before it stopped ringing.

"Jeffrey, it's me. I'm not sure, but it may be time. I know I felt something. Please hurry home. I need you to take me to the hospital."

He sensed the urgency in Jenny's voice and darted out of the office, brushing by John Calendar, who nodded at him, stone-faced.

Rushing home, he led Jenny out of the apartment and eased her into the car. She slid down in her seat, breathing heavily and placing her hands on the prominent bulge in her belly. Jeffrey darted furtive glances at her, remaining focused on the road. He nearly ran a red light in his haste. Finally, he pulled into the hospital parking lot. That strange, familiar feeling gripped him as he recalled his visits to his grandfather at the very same hospital. He wanted to run, but he knew Jenny could hardly walk. A panic gripped him.

For the first time, he began to worry about the baby's health. They checked in at the reception desk, where the volunteer immediately summoned a nurse's aid who promptly arrived with a wheelchair.

The elevator ride could not go fast enough. Jenny appeared pale and nervous; Jeffrey would not let his nervousness show. On the fifth floor, they heard the wailing as they passed the nursery. The aid parked the wheelchair in an examining room and went to summon a nurse. Jeffrey heard his heart pounding in his ears. Jenny began to draw deep breaths. He gripped her hand in his own. Commotion ensued. Doctors and nurses flew by in a flurry, bypassing them. More patients began pouring in. The hospital intercom paged one doctor after another. Jeffrey became frantic. Suddenly, he glanced down. Jenny's lap had become soaked. Jeffrey panicked, letting go of her hand and darting down the hallway. He wanted a doctor—any doctor, to attend to Jenny immediately.

He looked back over his shoulder at her. He could see her tearing up. He hoped only her water had broken. Out of the corner of his eye, he spied drops on the floor. She began to bleed profusely.

Suddenly, he came face to face with a doctor. He froze. Jeffrey instantly recognized the swarthy complexion, the gray hair, the mustache. The name tag read, "Dr. Mustafa." He stood face to face with the same doctor that had mysteriously restored his grandfather's health. At first, he feared exposing himself to one of the soul switchers. But his desperation to save his wife and unborn child overcame his fear. He grabbed the man by the shoulder and confronted him.

"I need your help, right away," Jeffrey glared at him with all the resolve he could muster.

"I'm sorry, but I'm not assigned to this floor. And this is not my specialty. I'm not an OBGYN."

"You're a doctor. You took an oath to save lives. I need you to save my wife and child's lives *now*," Jeffrey growled as he blocked his path.

"I'll page someone for you. I must go," Dr. Mustafa answered quietly and impassively.

Jeffrey shoved him against the wall and snarled at Dr. Mustafa.

"I know who you are, and I know what you can do. Now follow me."

The two men ran down the hall and into the maternity ward. No Jenny. A young nurse recognized Jeffrey and pointed to the delivery room. Both men donned masks and gloves. Jeffrey waved at the nurses and the intern.

"Clear the room."

Jeffrey comforted Jenny as Dr. Mustafa stood over her. He pulled the curtain around them and motioned for Jeffrey to extinguish the room lights. In seconds, the familiar whirring sound filled the room as the blue light enveloped Jenny. At that very moment, two floors below, an emergency room resident returned to the drug addicted patient the EMT's had just brought in, finding him still and lifeless, his eyes wide open.

Jenny slowly opened her eyes, searching for Jeffrey. He gently patted her brow with a damp towel. Smiling, he pointed to the baby resting comfortably on her breast. All seemed well at that moment, but he knew everything had a price. Jeffrey exited the room with Dr. Mustafa, bidding the nurse to go and look after Jenny. The two men walked down the hall silently, each knowing the other's secret. They quietly ducked into the empty lounge at the end of the hall. Jeffrey motioned to Dr. Mustafa to take a seat. The two men sized each other up like quarry and prey. Finally, Jeffrey spoke.

"I'm sorry I got rough with you."

Dr. Mustafa smiled and gestured.

"Desperate men do desperate things. No harm, no foul. So, we've met before. Refresh my memory."

Jeffrey stared into Dr. Mustafa's nearly black expressionless eyes.

"Yes. You saved my grandfather's life ten years ago. I saw what happened. So, what price will I have to pay for what I know and for what you have done tonight?"

Dr. Mustafa leaned forward in his chair, reached over and placed his right hand on Jeffrey's shoulder.

"You are correct. Knowledge can be expensive. It's how you use it that separates one man from the other. You kept this secret for ten years. I believe you will keep it for another ten. After that, who knows what will happen?"

Dr. Mustafa stood up, turned and headed for the door. Jeffrey reached out, placed his hand on the doctor's shoulder and spoke in a hushed undertone.

"How do I thank you?"

Dr. Mustafa turned to face him, placed his finger to his lips and replied,

"By your silence," and left the room.

Jeffrey turned his attention to his wife and child. The next day, they returned home. Both Jenny and Jeffrey rose to the occasion, tending to baby Jason's every need.

Upon returning to work, Jeffrey began to wonder whether Dr. Mustafa and John Calendar were closely connected. Both men bore the mark of the soul switchers. Jeffrey tried not to let his imagination run wild. Still, he began to play out various scenarios in his head. What if John Calendar became aware of what Jeffrey knew? Did it pose a threat to his family? To his job, his livelihood, his ability to support his family? Should he leave the firm, leave the city? He wrestled with the thought of sharing any of this with Jenny. She still had no idea what happened during her delivery in the hospital's maternity ward.

Just as he struggled with these thoughts, his office phone rang. The voice on the other end sent a jolt through him. John Calendar wanted to see him. Jeffrey steeled himself for the anticipated blow. He felt a twinge of weakness as he entered John Calendar's office. One never knew what to expect from him.

"So, Clyman, congratulations are in order. I heard you became a father. I trust everything went smoothly at the hospital."

It never sounded like a question when John Calendar posed one. Jeffrey stiffened up slightly, wondering what he knew. Was John Calendar testing him? Finally, Jeffrey responded in an ever so controlled manner.

"Yes, it did. The doctors at the hospital performed a near miracle. We greatly appreciate their skilled attention. It couldn't have gone better. Thank you for asking," Jeffrey replied.

Quarry and prey. Cat and mouse. Trained litigators. The same skill. Each of them read between the lines of the other's speech. Jeffrey waited for the proverbial other shoe to drop.

"That's all, Clyman; just wanted to check in and wish you the best. Glad you're back,"

John Calendar arose from his chair, turning to face the window.

"Oh, and one more thing. I would like to invite you to a gathering at my home Saturday evening. You and your bride, of course. Seven o'clock. We'll expect you."

Jeffrey remained confused. Why would John Calendar want to invite them to his home? He knew he had to go. How would he explain it to Jenny? Who would they trust as a babysitter for newborn Jason? These thoughts raced through his head on the drive home. When he arrived, he found Jenny putting the baby to sleep. She looked exhausted. Still, she led him to the kitchen where she had prepared a sumptuous dinner. Jeffrey began to unwind and relax as they enjoyed the dinner, until Jenny confronted him with a series of questions.

"What happened when I passed out in the hospital? Who was that wonderful doctor that delivered our baby? I want to send him a thank you note. How did you get him to help you?"

Jeffrey went pale. He could not tell Jenny that someone died so their baby could live. Worse yet, that he enlisted the aid of one of the soul switchers. He had to think fast.

"I guess we just got lucky. He happened to pass by and was kind enough to offer to help. I guess he could somehow tell we needed him. He knew just what to do. I'm sorry, but I didn't get his name," Jeffrey calmly responded.

When they settled down to sleep, Jenny's instincts began to kick in. A trained psychologist can pick up on a lie just as well as a trained lawyer can spin one. She switched on the light and turned to face Jeffrey.

"Now, tell me the truth. We don't keep secrets from each other—even to protect the ones we love. What really happened at the hospital?" Jenny confronted him, face to face.

"It's too fantastic for you to believe, really," he answered, reaching for the lamp.

She blocked his hand, stopping him.

"The truth, please."

Jeffrey knew that look. He had seen it at every one of his own therapy sessions when he was Jenny's patient. He had no choice. He told her every detail. She listened intently, then touched his face with her hand.

"And what do you plan to do?" she held his gaze.

"Do? What do you *think* I should do?" he asked.

"Don't answer a question with a question," she retorted flatly.

"I intend for us to go on with our lives, plain and simple—come what may. We still don't really know what these people are up to. We'll just have to see how it all plays out," Jeffrey tried to soothe her with a conciliatory tone.

"I said those words to you years ago when we first stumbled upon them. Things are different now. We're a family. You have to think of that," Jenny's annoyance seeped through her words.

"Believe me, I *am* thinking of that—every minute of every day. You need to trust that I will do the right thing," Jeffrey intoned.

Saturday night rolled around ever so quickly. Their next door neighbor Agnes agreed to watch the baby as Jeffrey and Jenny dressed for the occasion. Slightly on edge, they agreed to show up at the Calendar estate looking their very best. When they arrived, a valet parked their car. Both Jenny and Jeffrey found themselves slightly overwhelmed by the Calendar mansion. The butler took their coats and they followed him to the great room as the other guests appeared.

Jeffrey scanned the room with the precision of a sniper seeking his target. Every now and then, he would nudge Jenny and whisper in her ear as he recognized another high-level government official. Mayors, Governors, Congressman, Senators, Judges—he could hardly believe how high-level John Calendar's connections went. Then the thought struck him. How many of these people populated the ranks of the soul switchers? Jeffrey struggled with the thought that they reached so high into the fabric of society. He began to realize just how much control they could exert. Jenny sensed his uneasiness. Jeffrey knew it and seized the opportunity to slip away on the pretense of getting her a drink. Just as he did, he came face to face with the County Sheriff. No sign of recognition. Jeffrey wondered whether the man remembered their encounter in the diner over ten years ago.

As he strode across the room to the bar, Jeffrey turned back to see an elegant older woman addressing Jenny. He could not hear the words, but he studied Jenny's posture and discerned that she feigned a comfort level. Nothing genuine about her smile. She continued to listen, but he suspected she had little interest. Taking the champagne glasses from the bartender, Jeffrey swung around. The room dazzled him, with the huge crystal chandelier and the sparkling of the women's diamonds. He began to sift his way through the crowd, politely nodding as he approached Jenny. At that very moment, a man slipped between them, his back to Jeffrey. As Jeffrey approached, he recognized the man before he could turn around. He deftly stepped in between them, handing Jenny her drink and at the same time, smoothly extending his free hand.

"Jenny, this is the man who saved your life. Dr. Mustafa, you've met Jenny. I know she has waited anxiously for the opportunity to thank you," Jeffrey interceded.

Dr. Mustafa bowed, took Jenny's outstretched hand and kissed it, rather than shaking it. Jenny blushed, thanked him profusely and Jeffrey ushered her away. Still no sign of their host. The couple approached the roaring fire in the huge fireplace, admiring the books lining the built-in shelves flanking it. A waiter approached them with a tray of hot hors d'oeuvres. Both Jeffrey and Jenny politely declined. Turning, they witnessed the crowd in the room part like Moses's Red Sea. John Calendar appeared, flashing a smile as he brushed through the adoring crowd with a majestic gait. The room fell quiet all at once. John Calendar breezed past Jeffrey and Jenny, facing the mesmerized crowd. No one moved; no one spoke. John Calendar raised his glass, addressing the group.

"Tonight, we convene with a great purpose. We gather here to put the world at ease—to let everyone know our mission. We have set out to make this world a safer place. We have committed to that purpose and resolve to martial all of our resources behind this noble cause. We will give it our very last breath if we must."

Jeffrey, having witnessed the power of the soul switchers personally on three separate occasions, read between the lines of John Calendar's speech. He stood behind Jenny and placed his arms around her in a gesture of protection. He could feel her warmth. The crowd responded to John Calendar with a toast, then followed his lead. One by one, they filed towards the fireplace, tossing their empty glasses in. As each glass smashed, the remaining few drops of alcohol fed the fire as it flared up. Jeffrey wondered how the glasses didn't melt in the raging inferno. As he mused over the scene, he glanced up. John Calendar had left the room. Jeffrey's curiosity overcame him. He excused himself to Jenny and slipped away.

Jeffrey had no idea where the hallways would lead him. He just knew he had to follow his instincts. He stopped at each doorway and listened, until he heard the familiar voice. Slowly, he opened the study door a crack and squinted in with one eye. As he watched, John Calendar removed a handful of books from the shelf, reached in and the panel rotated. Jeffrey heard the familiar whirring sound followed by the blue glow. He stealthily slipped back down the hallway to the great room. The crowd seemed to have thinned out a bit. He scanned the room. No one seemed to notice his disappearance.

Suddenly, fear gripped him. He didn't see Jenny anywhere. He began approaching each of the women, asking if they had seen Jenny leave the room. His throat tightened. No one recalled seeing her leave the room. Jeffrey turned and swiftly left the room, again checking each room, listening at the door. Just then, Jenny emerged from a bathroom. Jeffrey embraced her with a sigh of relief. He took her by the hand and led her to the door of John Calendar's study. They peeked in. Jeffrey pulled her into the room behind him. Within seconds, John Calendar stood face to face with them, rotating the bookcase secret panel behind him. He didn't seem surprised. Instead, he motioned for them to sit across from his desk as he stood behind it.

"Yes, I know that you know. Why do you think I invited you? You will have a part in this, in time. Just not yet. We will reveal things to you—each thing when the time is right. No questions now, Mr. Clyman; no questions yet."

John Calendar addressed them like a preacher from the pulpit. He read the puzzled looks on their faces, then gestured toward the door. Jeffrey and Jenny arose from their chairs, returning to the great room arm in arm. The party scene began to wind down. They noticed a few of the guests heading down the hallway they just came from, rather than toward the front door. They eyed each other. They could not hold back. They waited, then quietly approached the study, checking to make sure no one had followed. Jeffrey peered in, then nodded to Jenny to follow him. They hung back, then hid behind the open closet door. The room had darkened. They watched as the guests they had followed entered the room behind the bookcase secret panel. They waited for what seemed like forever. None of them returned. Jeffrey grabbed Jenny's arm and they darted out of the room, heading for the front door. The butler retrieved their coats; the valet drove their car up and they headed into the night.

Jeffrey drove the ten miles from Westfield to Elizabeth City not uttering a word. Jenny kept falling asleep, then waking up with a start. He stopped the car abruptly when they reached their apartment building. Finally, Jeffrey broke the silence.

"It's some kind of a portal. I'm sure of it. I just don't know where it goes. I'm not sure I want to know."

Jenny slid towards him and looked him in the eye.

"You've already seen more than you should. And you work for this man. You have to see him every day. What do we do now?" Jenny pleaded.

Jeffrey turned off the engine, killed the headlights and stared out the windshield, shaking his head.

"I don't know. I just don't know what I'm *supposed* to do," his voice went monotonal.

That night they both fell into a deep but restless sleep.

Chapter III

1986

Jeffrey rolled over, searching for Jen. Hearing the rushing water from the shower pounding the tiles, he eased his way out of bed slowly. The aches and pains of middle age had begun to overtake him, along with thinning gray hair and the beginnings of a paunch. Jen had already seen their son safely off to school. Jeffrey staggered into the bathroom, throwing cold water on his face. Jen sang from inside the shower, turned it off and wrapped the towel he offered around herself. Their new home had plenty of room. They joked about the bathroom having more room than the living room of their old apartment. Jeffrey admired Jen's sleek, tight body and smooth skin as she let the towel drop to the floor. She caught his glance and playfully poked him in the ribs.

"It's off to work we go, counselor."

He pulled her up against him until he could feel her heartbeat.

"Maybe I'll just have to call in sick."

"Or maybe not," she teased, gently stroking the stubble on his face.

Jen slipped past Jeffrey and headed for the bedroom as he studied her.

Minutes later, Jeffrey fired up the engine of his new car. The radio came on, news story after news story. One becomes jaded after a while. First violent street gangs; then the rapid spread of the AIDS epidemic; political corruption—it all became garbled noise. Jeffrey switched the station. More of the same. The stories rained on the parade of an idyllic suburban paradise. But paradise could get boring after a while. Jeffrey's mind drifted back to his case load at the firm. As one of the senior partners now, John Calendar had entrusted some of the most high-profile cases to Jeffrey. He had to defend an oil company accused of polluting, a corporate executive charged with embezzlement and a labor official suspected of racketeering. A few cases never made it to his desk, however. Jeffrey sensed the pattern. All of the political corruption cases stayed on John Calendar's desk. The conclusion appeared obvious. John Calendar had to protect all of his friends in high places—the soul switchers. He needed them to carry out his plan.

Jeffrey had long since stopped worrying about the soul switchers. Every now and then his curiosity piqued. He still could not quite discern their overarching plan, but he trusted that they did not have nefarious intentions. The day wore on; he felt the tension in the back of his neck as it tightened up. Jeffrey thought about his next vacation—definitely on an island beach. In his younger days, he had experienced the serenity of the Caribbean, noticing the total absence of stress in the lifestyle. At the time, he wondered why anyone would ever return to the frenetic pace we live each day. Still, like everyone else he knew, he had done just that. His whole life seemed to amount to a set of trade-offs. The thought haunted him as he packed up his briefcase, locked his office door, slung his suit jacket over his shoulder and walked toward the elevator. Just then, his mind flashed back to the memory of that day when Janelle the receptionist found herself captive by that very same elevator.

Arriving home, Jeffrey swung the front door open as Jason flung himself at him, locking his arms around Jeffrey's neck. Jen poked her head out of the kitchen, smiling.

"Easy there, cowboy. You don't want to knock dad over—not if you want him to take you on that bicycle trip he promised for this weekend," Jen cautioned.

"Hey, big guy. Missed me?" Jeffrey studied his son's adoring gaze.

Jason nodded. Jeffrey placed his arm on the boy's shoulder and led him into the kitchen.

"So, tell me about your day. Did you fight any dragons? Make any pirates walk the plank? Or just fly around town on your space craft?" Jeffrey teased.

"No. I went to the playground with my friends. But I did see that man again. You know, the one I told you about. He wasn't scary, just kind of odd," Jason offered.

Jeffrey settled into a kitchen chair. Jen swung around after hearing Jason.

"Tell us a little more about this man. What does he look like? Was he walking, or did he drive a car? Did he approach you and your friends? Did he talk to you?" Jeffrey naturally went into cross-examining mode.

"No, he never says anything. He just watches us—sort of stares and then leaves. He's always alone and dresses weird," Jason confided.

"Weird? How's that?" Jen joined the conversation cautiously, so as not to intimidate Jason.

"He looks like his clothes are out of style or something," Jason struggled to explain.

Jeffrey and Jen exchanged knowing glances. They both suspected the soul switchers. The thought that they might be keeping watch on their son made them both uneasy. They decided to drop the conversation, since no harm had come of the incident.

"Remember, you have a doctor's appointment tomorrow morning, Jason, so don't jump off of any bridges, okay?" Jeffrey teased.

Jeffrey sank into his favorite living room chair. Glancing over at Jason, he remembered their last visit with Dr. Greeley. The doctor leaned on his elbows and peered over the top of his half glasses as he explained to Jeffrey and Jen that their son, although high functioning, may never lead a "normal" life. Jeffrey probed inquisitively, wondering if medical science didn't have some miracle cure—or at least a viable therapy for Jason's condition.

"Jason may well surprise us all, Dr. Greeley offered. As you know, we've done exhaustive testing and he does show great promise. But you see, the brain sometimes does peculiar things. While he can perform well in some areas, Jason may not progress in others. I'm reluctant to put a label on his condition just yet," Dr. Greeley smiled at them.

To Jen and Jeffrey, Jason appeared like any normal child at birth. He seemed to have some developmental issues later. They revolved around maturity. Still, he exhibited well above average intelligence and a heightened "sixth sense" perception.

Jeffrey snapped back to the present as the aroma of Jen's cooking wafted its way into the living room. He eyed Jason at the table, drawing. He decided to amble over and peer over his shoulder.

"So, buddy, what's this, a spaceship?" Jason pointed to an object in the picture.

Jason nodded. He had an uncanny talent for drawing.

"And who is this guy, a space alien?" Jeffrey treaded lightly as he probed.

He had learned from Jen that children's drawings often reveal their inner mental and emotional state.

Jason looked up at Jeffrey with a touch of fear in his eyes.

"They look like us, but they're really not."

"I see; and where do they come from?" Jeffrey asked.

"Another time," Jason offered, still transfixed on his drawing.

"You want to tell me about it later?" Jeffrey queried.

"No. I mean they *come from* a different time," Jason replied, matter-of-factly.

"And how did you know that?" Jeffrey continued to drill down.

"From my dreams. I saw them in my dreams," Jason turned and appeared disturbed.

Jen approached the dining room table from the kitchen, feigning interest in the drawing. She had overheard the conversation and felt compelled to weigh in. After all, this touched her both personally and professionally.

"So, what happened in your dream, Jason?" Jen placed her hand on his shoulder.

"They came into my room, looking for me," Jason seemed slightly agitated.

"Did they frighten you?" Jen rubbed his shoulders gently, in an effort to relax Jason, as she looked over at Jeffrey with a troubled expression.

"Only a little, 'cause I didn't know who they were or what they wanted," Jason responded, calmly.

"Did they tell you what they wanted?" Jen leaned over Jason.

"No. They just kept coming back and watching me," Jason shrugged his shoulders.

"Did any of the people in the dream look like the man in the park?" Jen began to probe more deeply.

"Yeah. One of them was him," Jason pointed to a man with a mustache in the drawing.

Jeffrey placed his finger on his lips, signaling to Jen to let it go. He did not want to upset Jason. Just then Jason crumpled up the drawing, ran into the kitchen and threw it in the garbage.

"That was a very good drawing. You don't want to keep it?" Jeffrey inquired.

Jason shook his head.

"No. I don't want them watching me anymore," he replied.

Jeffrey and Jen exchanged glances.

"That's probably a good idea, then," Jen ran her hands through Jason's hair.

That night everyone in the Clyman household turned in early, in anticipation of the doctor's appointment the next morning. And the dreams came, one after another, like the coming attractions before the film at the movies. Unbeknownst to each of them, they had the same dream. The soul switchers came; they took the souls of the unworthy and breathed life back into the deserving ones clinging to life. But they never threatened or harmed Jeffrey, Jen or Jason.

Morning rolled around and everyone gathered at the breakfast table. Jason poured out his favorite cereal; Jen fried eggs and Jeffrey consumed a banana. No one spoke at first. Then, as they finished eating, Jason spoke up, pencil in hand and ready to draw.

"They came again last night," he announced.

"Did they, now?" Jeffrey tried to keep the mood light, knowing full well his son had a disturbing dream.

"Did anything different happen this time?" Jen leaned in to Jason.

"Yeah. I saw a blue light and I heard a weird noise," Jason confided.

Jeffrey had to contain himself. How could his son know about the soul switchers when he had never seen them? He motioned to Jen to let the conversation go.

Dr. Greeley lifted his hand, circling around Jason and asked him to follow it with his eyes without moving his head. Jason dutifully obeyed. Then he had Jason up and walking across the exam room. The usual standard set of tests continued until Jason slumped into the chair. Jen wrapped her arms around his shoulders from behind. Jeffrey looked on, waiting for Dr. Greeley to make some pronouncement.

"He's fine. Nothing has changed that I can see. No sense doing any more diagnostic work if Jason feels okay and is functioning fine. I do have one more question. Does he have any disturbing dreams?"

Jeffrey, Jen and Jason felt the words slash through them simultaneously. Taken by surprise, they had no time to hide their reactions.

"I see, I see", remarked Dr. Greeley. "I don't believe in medication for such things. Let's just wait and see if they continue. You'll let me know," he nodded and extended his hand to shake Jason's.

Visibly disturbed, Jason shuffled out of the exam room and down the corridor with his head down. Jeffrey and Jen could feel his tension. They felt compelled to address the problem, but not sure who to turn to. Definitely not the neurologist. Jen thought about her former colleagues that practiced child psychology, but she wanted to keep the problem discreet. Jeffrey felt Jason needed someone he would trust to talk about the dreams. The phenomenon of a shared dream changed the landscape. They all had a stake in this. Silent for now, Jeffrey and Jen knew they would take up the conversation themselves when Jason went to sleep.

A pounding rain beat down on the roof of the Clyman home that night. Ghostly shadows emerged from the headlights of passing cars. Then the thunder struck, followed by the lightning. Jason pulled his blankets over his head. The piercing light penetrated; the crack of the thunder seemed ever so close. Unseen, a lone figure plodded through the rivulets of rain, approaching the Clyman house. Jason began to drift off to sleep. The figure came closer, still undetected. Jeffrey wrapped his arms around Jen's waist as they both fell into a deep sleep.

As the shadowy figure approached the rays of the streetlight, it split in two. Not one, but two figures sloshed through the rain, squished through the mud and came to rest under the rear window. One last flash of lightning illuminated them for a split second. Still unseen, they appeared to disappear. Jason finally stopped his nervous tossing and turning under the blankets and felt the veil of sleep overtake him. Suddenly, he threw the blankets off, opened his eyes wide and gasped at the two shadowy figures. He let out a cry. They were gone.

Jeffrey leapt out of bed upon hearing Jason's cry and ran across the hall to his room. Jason clutched his blanket, shaking as Jeffrey switched on the light.

"Bad dream, tiger?"

"No, it was real. They were here," Jason muttered.

Jeffrey dropped down on the bed beside Jason to comfort him.

"I'm sure it seemed real, but—"

"It *was* real. They *were* here. I was awake. I know it," Jason blurted out.

Jen poked her head into the room, tying the belt on her robe.

"What can I get you boys?" she asked.

"It's okay. We've got it under control," Jeffrey assured her.

"No, we don't," Jason insisted.

Jeffrey motioned for her to go back to bed.

"Okay. I believe you. Someone was here. So, what did they want?" Jeffrey queried.

"I dunno", Jason wiped a tear away. "But I don't want them coming back," he asserted.

"Well, you just call out to me loud and clear if they do," Jeffrey wrapped the blanket tightly around Jason.

"Okay. I will. You promise?"

"I promise. You call; I come," Jeffrey assured him.

Jeffrey returned to Jen.

"What do we do? This is really disturbing him," Jeffrey sighed.

"I've got an idea. One of my colleagues from graduate school did some unusual work—fringe stuff: you know, psychics, past life regression. Some of it is for real. It's just not accepted by mainstream practitioners. I'm going to call her in the morning," Jen closed her eyes with that pronouncement.

Jeffrey needed to focus on his increasing case load at the firm. He needed to trust Jen's instincts to handle Jason's problem. Still, his son's unrest gnawed at him. More and more, he was convinced that it had some connection to the soul switchers. But what would they possibly want with a special needs ten-year-old boy? Jeffrey shrugged off the thought as he prepared for his next court appearance.

After school, Jen picked Jason up and drove him to her friend, Dr. Sharah. Jason nervously tapped on his school textbooks for most of the trip. Normally, he liked to play with the car radio, searching the dial for his favorite songs to sing along with. Not today. When they arrived at the building, Jason studied the architecture.

"It looks like a church."

"That's because it used to be a church. Then the church people built a new, bigger church and they made the old church into offices. You'll like Dr. Sharah. She's different," Jen soothed Jason.

"Different? Different how?" Jason turned to her.

"You'll see. Just different than anyone you've ever met—in a good way," Jen reassured him.

They entered the old church. Jason looked up at the vaulted ceilings, scanning the religious images on the stained-glass windows. Everything smelled musty. He did not feel comforted. They went down a corridor behind the stage to a row of office doors. Jen knocked. A woman in a long patterned dress with a sash and a turban answered the door, smiling at Jen. The two women embraced. Jen turned to Jason.

"This is my very dear friend, Dr. Sharah—"

"Felicity. Please call me Felice," she extended her hand to Jason and motioned for them to come in.

The office smelled of incense; the curtains were drawn and large candles in glasses burned on the table. They sank into a couch, side by side as Felice settled into her rocking chair. A cat jumped on her lap for a moment, then sprang off and hid in the corner.

"So, Jason, your mother tells me you are a very special boy. I need to find out for myself just how special you are. So, with your permission, I want to do some experiments. Do you like experiments?" Felice leaned over, smiling. Her dark complexion and hair glistened.

Jason nodded.

She knew she had begun to win his trust.

"All right, then. Let's begin."

Dr. Sharah reached down under the table and placed a series of metal boxes on top. She pointed to each box, gesturing with her hand.

"Now, as I point to each box, I want you to tell me if there is anything in it. If so, try and tell me what's inside. Any questions?" Dr. Sharah waited, then began to point to the boxes, one by one.

"Nothing in that one. Something in this one. Something sharp that doesn't belong. Next one has something with wheels. Last one, I'm not sure," Jason replied emphatically.

"You did quite well, Jason; quite well indeed,"

Dr. Sharah reached in and withdrew a kitchen knife from the second box and a toy car from the third box. She raised the first one, revealing the emptiness. When she opened the last box, she held up a mirror.

"So, Jason, how did you know what was in the boxes?" Dr. Sharah inquired.

"I don't know; I just knew," Jason responded.

After a series of tests, Dr. Sharah wrote a few notes on a lined pad and peered over her half eyeglasses at Jen.

"Heightened perception. He has ESP. It will most likely become more intense as time goes on. As for the dreams, we will need to have another session to explore that. Will that be okay with you?" she turned to Jason.

"I guess. I'm a little scared, but I want to know why I'm having them. And they're not all dreams," Jason took the two women by surprise.

"We will call you and make another appointment," Jen assured Dr. Sharah, rising from the couch and leaning over to hug her.

Jason remained silent for most of the ride home, eyes transfixed on the road ahead. The traffic light changed; Jason turned to Jen with a sudden look of fear across his face.

"Don't go!" he shouted, as a car raced across the intersection.

Jen's heart raced; she reached over and held Jason before accelerating.

"How did you know he would do that?" she held his gaze.

She began to understand what Dr. Sharah meant about Jason's heightened perception. Somehow, he anticipated the other driver's move. Jen began to wonder just what other strange and curious ways Jason's abilities would manifest themselves as time went on. How would she impart the knowledge to Jeffrey? What would he think? They were two very pragmatic people that never even considered things like psychic phenomena. If anything, the revelation secretly scared

Jen. As the days passed, she even found herself pulling away from Jason emotionally, as a means of self-preservation. She found herself conflicted in her roles of psychologist and mother.

As the fall weather set in, the Clymans took advantage of it. Frequent weekend outings brought them to hiking and camping in the woods and enjoying the trails. On one of these outings, Jeffrey caught his first glimpse of Jason's special abilities. It seems that the more aware Jason became of his talents, the more he exercised control over them. They had just pitched their tent when Jason emerged and shook his head, as if to say 'no.'

"What's the matter, big guy?" Jeffrey asked.

"Not a good place. We have to move. Over there," Jason was emphatic.

He had pointed to a clearing off in the distance. It would require them to disassemble the tent, pack up all of their supplies and carry them quite a long way. Jason persisted, stamping his foot and pointing, while shaking his head. Reluctantly, Jeffrey and Jen followed his lead. Hours later, after eating, the Clyman family tucked themselves in to their sleeping bags. Upon awakening, Jason nudged Jeffrey and Jen. He motioned for them to exit the tent. As they did, he handed them the binoculars. Jeffrey peered through them as the shafts of morning light began to pierce through the trees. There, in the very spot where they had originally pitched the tent, a bear had torn up what remained of someone else's campsite. Jason shrugged his shoulders, as if to say, "I told you so."

Jeffrey and Jen would hold late night discussions in bed after Jason went to sleep, discussing his unusual and heightened perception. Jen continued to take Jason to Dr. Sharah for more tests and "experiments", as she called them. Jason began to show signs of boredom. They still had not yet fully addressed his dreams. The time had come to confront them.

Dr. Sharah unrolled a large sheet of paper and handed Jeffrey a set of colored markers. Before she could give him any instructions, he began to draw, almost automatically. Both women kept their distance, so as not to interfere or influence Jason. He picked up his pace. Jen and Felice looked at one another knowingly. Jason revealed his fears through his drawing. His innermost haunting thoughts and preoccupations took on a life of their own on paper. When he finished, Jason sank back, as if his energy level had declined dramatically.

Dr. Sharah peered over the top of her glasses. Leaning forward, she began to trace the objects and the figures on the paper. She turned to Jason.

"Tell me about your dreams."

"They come into my room. They just stand there. I can't see their faces. They just watch me. Then they leave. Sometimes there's a blue light and a noise."

Jen gripped the arm of the couch. She remembered the night when she and Jeffrey hid in the library at John Calendar's mansion. But how could Jason know about the soul switchers? He never saw them. Or did he? Jen began to believe that maybe Jason did not dream every encounter. Dr. Sharah nodded and gently probed, encouraging Jason to go on.

"They watch me when I go to the park with my friends. They never say anything. And they wear odd clothes—like they're out of style."

Jen knew she would have to call Dr. Sharah and have a private conversation, but she wanted to hear what she had to say.

"Jason, you see, your dreams are the playground for your mind. That's where your mind gets to freely think and feel without you stopping it. It's a place for you to work out whatever bothers you while you are awake. But you must understand, what you see in your dreams is not always what it appears to be. Do you follow me?" Dr. Sharah raised her eyebrows, soliciting his response.

"Yeah, but these are real. The dreams are the same all the time and I know they're not just dreams. I see them when I'm awake, too," Jason insisted.

Dr. Sharah took Jason's hand and held it tightly.

"I know. I know. They *are* real. So, here's what I want you to tell me. What do you *feel* when you experience the encounters with these people?" Dr. Sharah held his gaze.

"I'm scared because I don't know who they are, and I don't know what they want. Why don't they go away?" Jason's voice sounded strained.

"We will find that out in time. Let's keep working on it," Dr. Sharah reassured Jason.

"I'll call you," Jen nodded to Felice, leaving hurriedly.

One day when Jason had a holiday with no school, Jen overheard him humming as he drew at the dining room table. She glanced over from her work in the kitchen, noticing him increasing his pace, letting out grunts and groans, seemingly agitated. She approached carefully. Jason slowly turned to her, his face appearing pained.

"What's the matter, sweetheart?" she queried.

"She's gonna die. Aunt Sally is going to die," he tore the drawing in half with a violent gesture, glaring at Jen.

"Jason! Why would you say a thing like that? Everyone's going to die some time," Jen returned the glare.

"No. She is going to die *today*!" Jason pounded on the table.

"Jason, I think you had better go to your room and take a time-out. You need to think about what you said," Jen pointed down the hallway.

Just as Jason began to plod toward his room, the telephone rang. Jen answered it. She nearly dropped it seconds later, as the voice on the other end broke the news that her great-aunt Sally had just passed away within the hour. Jen hung up the phone, sinking into a kitchen chair, her head in her hands.

Jen tried not to overburden Jeffrey with the details of their sessions with Dr. Sharah. At the same time, she knew the importance of keeping Jeffrey apprised of Jason's emerging 'talents'. Weeks went by; the sessions continued and both Jeffrey and Jen noticed Jason's unrest. After a long weekend outing, the Clyman household seemed unusually quiet for a Monday morning. Jeffrey peered into Jason's room, ready to give him the nudge to get up for school. He stared at the empty bed for a moment. No one in the bathroom either. The backyard? Empty. He even checked the garage. No Jason. The backpack remained on the chair. Worried, he stood in the doorway as Jen sat up in bed. She could read the expression on his face.

"What is it? What's happened?" she blurted out.

"Jason's gone," Jeffrey blurted out, shaking his head in disbelief.

"What do you mean, *gone*? Jen sprang out of bed and grabbed her robe.

"I looked everywhere. I can't find him. He would never leave for school without his backpack. It's still in his room," Jeffrey became even more agitated.

In minutes, the Clyman residence buzzed with police detectives. Curious neighbors made their way to the front door.

"Ma'am, does your son ever wander off? Does he have a favorite place to go, to play; does he ever hide out anywhere?" sergeant Wheeler clicked his pen and scribbled notes on his pad.

Jen could not hold back her tears as Jeffrey tried to console her.

"No signs of forced entry; we'll dust for fingerprints. You're sure he didn't just decide to skip school or anything like that? You said he's a special needs kid. They do sometimes take off unsupervised, don't they?" Sergeant Wheeler's words just rubbed salt in the wound.

"You called the school, and he hasn't shown up there yet either?" Sergeant Wheeler put his pad and pen back in the pocket of his trench coat as Jen shook her head.

"We'll call you the minute we hear anything. I promise," Sergeant Wheeler did his best to muster what passed for compassion.

Jeffrey nearly tripped down the front steps as he left for work, nervous and exhausted. How would he concentrate on anything *but* his son's disappearance? Still, he knew he could not stay home—even to comfort Jen. Pulling into the parking lot at the law firm, he nearly clipped the car next to him when he threw his door open. He had to get control of himself. He could not let his co-workers—and certainly not John Calendar, see him like this. No sooner than he flung his coat over the back of his office chair, the intercom on his desk phone buzzed. John Calendar summoned him to his office.

"I understand you had some difficulty this morning, Clyman?" he swiveled around in his chair to face Jeffrey.

"Yes, sir. It's my son. He's gone missing," Jeffrey's voice trembled. The words seemed so surreal.

"Call your wife and tell her everything will be all right," John Calendar pointed to his phone.

"And how do you know this?" Jeffrey's voice became embittered.

"The boy is safe. He's in good hands," John Calendar uttered the words dispassionately.

Jeffrey felt his face flush as he drew himself up to face his boss.

"What have you done with him? Where is my son?" Jeffrey glared at John Calendar.

"I told you that all things would be revealed to you in good time. That time is near. Bring your wife to my home this evening. We will explain everything then," John Calendar advised.

His boss's revelation did nothing to comfort him. Jeffrey turned around, grabbed his coat from his office and left. Returning home, he found Jen still in the kitchen, staring out the window. He could read the guilt on her face. He dropped down in front of her and gave her the news.

"They abducted him? They kidnapped our son! What are you going to do about it?" Jen lashed out at Jeffrey.

It took over an hour, but Jeffrey finally calmed Jen down. Her energy spent, she leaned on him and crumpled onto the bed. Jeffrey sat by her side until evening.

Jeffrey and Jen drove through the Calendar mansion's gates. The butler greeted them, offering to take their coats.

"That won't be necessary. Just take us to Mr. Calendar, please," Jeffrey demanded.

They entered the study. John Calendar arose from his chair, strode out from behind his desk, extending his hand in as much of a gesture of welcoming hospitality as he was capable of. Jeffrey advanced toward him, barely containing his hostility.

"Where is our son, and what have you done with him?"

Jen glared at John Calendar like a cat poised to strike.

"You know, Jason is a very special boy. We would certainly never harm him. We just need his special abilities. I told you we would reveal everything to you. You know what we do; you just don't know quite why. I will tell you now," John Calendar motioned to Jeffrey and Jen to each take a seat. He then poured a glass of Scotch for each of them.

"Years ago, a group of men came together to save the world. To save it from what, you ask? To save it from itself. They knew then that those who did not value human life would soon destroy it for everyone else. So, they set out to preserve the lives of the deserving. You've already seen how we do it. We all want the same thing—to live life to the fullest, with no regrets." John Calendar stopped abruptly. He sensed Jeffrey's agitation.

"So, what does that have to do with my son? He's an innocent ten-year-old boy. He needs his family around him," Jeffrey nearly growled the words.

"As you know, our people have special abilities. You already know that we transfer the souls of the undeserving to those deserving individuals that are clinging to life. And you know that we are time travelers. This is not a perfect science yet. We still have more to learn if we are to accomplish our mission," John Calendar took a draught of his Scotch.

"And just what is your mission?" Jeffrey hissed back at him.

"You could say, to rid the world of the scourge—to finally learn from and not repeat the mistakes of the past," John Calendar sat back in his chair.

"Jason's abilities may help us. He will not be harmed. I give you my word," John Calendar leaned forward and gestured.

"You must see the big picture here. The world has become a dangerous place. It doesn't have to remain that way. We can stop it, but we need your help," John Calendar responded in his usual manner—never a request; always a demand.

"How long?" Jen piped up.

"Just a few more days. We need to see if Jason's abilities are developed enough yet. If they are, we will bring him back later to carry out the next phase of our plan. If not, we're done with him."

Jeffrey and Jen looked at one another, then arose and turned their backs on John Calendar, heading for the door. Not one word spoken.

Three days passed. Three sleepless nights passed, with Jeffrey and Jen tossing, turning, watching the hours slowly turn on the alarm clock. Both of them sat nervously poised by the phone, by the door, waiting for some sign. The only phone call came from the detectives. They had no leads. Jeffrey and Jen did not let on that they knew anyone connected with the abduction. They could not bring themselves to call it a kidnapping. Jeffrey refused to go to the office. He could not stand the thought that his boss masterminded his son's abduction. Then, as suddenly as he disappeared, the front door opened, and Jason ran to them. Overwhelmed, Jeffrey and Jen held him. They could hardly believe the ordeal had ended. Stunned, they just stared at Jason—as if they weren't sure it was really him. Finally, Jeffrey dropped to his knees. Jen held Jason at arm's length. Jeffrey spoke first.

"What happened, son? Where did they take you?"

"I was here. I was here all the time. But you weren't here. This house was here, but different people lived in it. There was an old car in the driveway," Jason jumped from one sentence to the next, in a staccato beat, half out of breath.

"It's okay. It's okay. You're here now, with us. It's over. It's over and you're home," Jen reassured and comforted Jason.

Jeffrey and Jen exchanged that knowing glance that comes with the years as couples grow together. Jason had time traveled. The concept of living in the same place at a different time seemed so alien to both of them. Why would the soul switchers need a ten-year-old special needs child to carry out their plan? They wanted to know more but felt it best to leave well enough alone and not risk upsetting Jason. They all needed to get on with their lives.

Chapter IV

1996

John Calendar paced back and forth in his home office—something never seen in his office at the law firm. Even with all the forces on his side, he had fallen behind schedule. He needed to accelerate the plan while maintaining the delicate balance, keeping the visibility of the soul switchers below the radar, so to speak. As much as he felt in control, he had to accept the bitter reality that certain forces trumped his best efforts. Another round of extreme sunspot activity and solar flares held his plans at bay. They could not risk sending any of their operatives through the portals. They could perish. The sunspot activity came at an inopportune time. The soul switchers needed to expand their activity beyond North America. Strangely, the solar flares arrived in the dead of winter. John Calendar snarled as he reported back to the high command, dropping into his high-backed desk chair.

Just two towns away, Jeffrey and Jason listened intently to the radio. New Jersey's Governor Whitman had closed the roads to all except emergency personnel. A two-foot snowstorm dumped its wrath on the Garden State, grinding everyone and every thing to a halt. Only police, fire, ambulances, doctors and nurses could travel—if they could even navigate the treacherous roads. It would take hours to clear anything but the major highways. Jeffrey and Jason suited up in their winter gear, grabbed their shovels and began the long process of digging out the family's cars from the driveway. It took the better part of the day just to clear the driveway, the walkway and the front steps. Jen peered out every now and then on the scene, as she prepared a hot meal for them.

Jeffrey carefully eyed Jason as they worked. His son had overcome many of his special need's challenges, but still seemed unable to live completely independently. At the same time, his special talents and abilities continued to amaze everyone he came in contact with. This posed a conundrum for Jeffrey and Jen. They wanted Jason to continue with his education but could not send him away to school.

After a time, the whirling snow began to take its toll on Jeffrey's energy level. The cold penetrated his clothes; his soaked gloves made his hands ache; and the soreness began to overtake his back muscles as he piled the snow higher and higher. Jason seemed unaffected by the effort. Finally, the two men stopped, leaning on their shovels. A bright sun began to warm them as they headed inside the house to thaw out.

Jeffrey had begun to feel his age. Largely sedentary these days, he had grown accustomed to letting Jason perform most of the home maintenance chores. Somehow, he did not have the energy in his fifties that he had in his forties. He could not deny that he had reached a turning point. Age began to tighten its grip on him.

The hot meal Jen prepared hit the spot for both Jason and Jeffrey. Afterwards, Jeffrey built a blazing fire in the fireplace. All three of them sat on the living room couch, watching the streetlights glisten on the snow as it began to freeze over. Nothing stirred. Jeffrey began to doze off. Jason and Jen left him on the couch as they cleaned up the dishes. Jeffrey lapsed into a deep sleep and began to dream profusely. He re-lived Jason's abduction, Jen's near miscarriage, his grandfather's death—and then saw himself pulled into the soul switcher's portal, whirled into darkness as the blue light faded. His anxiety level peaked. Suddenly, he felt a pain in his left arm and a crushing weight on his chest—the classic symptoms of a heart attack. He awoke, his brow sweating. The sensations continued. He was not dreaming. Jeffrey let out a yell. Jen and Jason came running. Jen sent Jason for the phone, furiously dialing for an ambulance. How would they ever get to Jeffrey in time? Thoughts raced through Jen's head. Finally, silently, the ambulance skidded around the corner, lights flashing. Jason and Jen grabbed their coats. Only one of them could ride with him. Jen sent Jason inside.

"Just stay by the phone. I will call you as soon as I know anything," she shouted as she slammed the front door behind her.

Hours passed. Jen sat rooted in the chair by Jeffrey's side in the emergency room. The sound of the oxygen and the beeping of the tracer overtook her every thought. She gripped his cold hand in hers. His eyes began to close. The din of the hospital staff scurrying around faded into the background. Neither Jeffrey nor Jen regularly observed any religious practice or ritual. At a time like this, one's faith gets put to the test. Jen repeated a silent prayer to herself, hoping it would be heard. She had never experienced the tension of watching anyone close to her clinging to life. The thought rushed into her head. What if Jeffrey didn't survive? How would she give Jason the attention he needed? At that split second, a man in surgical scrubs pulled back the curtain. In spite of the hospital garb, she quickly recognized him. The same Dr. Mustafa that saved her own life peered over at Jeffrey, then smiled knowingly at Jen. She knew then, Jeffrey would not die.

After what seemed like an eternity, a nurse's aide came in and began to move Jeffrey's bed. Jen followed him to the elevator. Arriving in the cardiac unit, she settled into the chair by Jeffrey's side once again. One after another, doctors, nurses and nurses' aides shuffled in, checking Jeffrey's vital signs, taking his blood and scribbling down notes from readings they took on the machines. Finally, Jen found the strength to amble over to the nurse's station and ask for the charge nurse. A moment later, a large woman with a Jamaican accent appeared. Nurse Roma Brightman came out from behind the counter. She placed one large arm around Jen to comfort her.

"He is going to be just fine, just fine, I assure you. His vital signs are strong; his will is strong, and he has remained conscious. These are good omens. He will have the best of care. Now, you go on down and get yourself something to eat in the cafeteria. I will look in on him myself," she raised her eyebrows to elicit a response from Jen.

"I'll be back up shortly. Thank you so very much," Jen choked to get the words out as she weakly found her way to the elevator.

Jen nearly fell asleep as she finished the cup of soup. Her head buzzed. Her knees felt weak. She remembered that she had promised to call Jason. Leaving the cafeteria, she spotted the telephones.

"Hi, it's me. He's okay. We have to wait for his test results. It could take a long time. No, you stay put. I can't have you driving on those icy roads. I'll keep you posted as soon as I know anything. See if you can get an updated weather report, okay?" Jen gently let the receiver go.

Just then, those chilling words came over the hospital's public address system.

"Code blue; code blue..."

A group of teenagers stopped right in front of her, shouting. She could not hear what room they had announced. Fear overcame Jen. She dashed toward the elevators. The gang of teens slid into the elevator ahead of her and began randomly pushing buttons. Jen glared at them.

"This is a hospital! People are sick and dying here. A little respect and decorum would go a long way," she snapped.

The teens looked back and forth at one another and fell silent. Jen hit the elevator button again for the cardiac unit. The distraction had derailed her attention. She ran out of the elevator, heading for Jeffrey's room. Too late. Panic set in as she stared at the empty space where he had been. She ran to the nurse's station. A petite Asian nurse pointed toward an operating room without even looking up from her phone call. Jen sailed down the hall, nearly upsetting the phlebotomist's cart full of blood specimens. She pounded on the double doors to the operating room. A nurse peered through the window at her, motioned for her to stand back and pushed the button to let her in.

Upon entering, the nurse handed Jen a cap, gown, gloves and a mask. Donning them quickly, she followed the nurse to the viewing window just outside of the operating room. Jen began to perspire profusely. Her heart pounded in her ears. She could barely make out Jeffrey's outline as doctors and nurses hovered over him. Panic overtook her. She darted glances around the anteroom, but could not find the nurse who let her in. The sight of blood spurting in and out of tubes nearly unhinged her. She felt the urge to vomit but stopped herself. She had to keep it together for Jeffrey. She could not tell what transpired as they labored over him. She knew it did not look good. She tried to see the numbers on the monitors, but the window in front of her had become fogged and clouded up. In desperation, she ran out and back down the hallway to the Cardiac Care nurse's station. Out of breath, she leaned over the counter and grabbed the nurse by the arm.

"My husband is on the operating table now. He needs help. You've got to help me—help *him*. You must page Dr. Mustafa. He knows how to help him," Jen shrieked.

The startled nurse dropped her clipboard and began to nervously thumb through her directory. A minute later, she shook her head.

"We don't have a Dr. Mustafa in this hospital. Perhaps he used to work here, but no longer does. Is he a cardiologist?" the nurse attempted to stay calm in an effort to calm Jen down.

"What? I don't know. I saw him here earlier this evening. Check again, please!" Jen implored her.

The nurse picked up her phone, dialed an extension and waited.

"I'll get the charge nurse for you. Perhaps she can help," the nurse assured Jen.

No nurse came. Jen could not wait any longer. She flew back down the hall and pounded on the doors again. The same nurse as before let her in, reluctantly. Jen confronted her.

"What is going on with my husband? What are you people doing for him? He can't die," Jen began to hyperventilate.

The nurse eased her down into a chair and attempted to console her.

"Trust me, ma'am. This team knows what it is doing. They are the best. He needs surgery. He apparently has a blocked artery. They're doing a bypass. His chances are very good. He has lost a lot of blood, though," the nurse's words calmed Jen enough for her to regain her strength.

Jen began to think of Jason. What would she tell him? How long should she wait to call him? Would he worry more if he knew his father's condition, or if he didn't hear from her? The nurse suggested she wait in the sitting room down the hall. Jen would not move. Not until she knew Jeffrey had come through the operation. Another two hours passed. Finally, one of the surgeons emerged. Mopping his brow, he approached Jen. She searched his face for a sign.

"Mrs. Clyman, I'm pleased to say your husband made it. He's out of the woods, but he will need some time to heal. He'll be in the recovery room. You should come back in about an hour. You can see him then. The anesthesia should wear off by then," Dr. Francis extended his gloved hand to Jen. She threw her arms around him.

"Thank you; thank you," Jen exclaimed.

The walk down a hospital hallway always seems like an eternity. The thoughts that run through people's heads as they wait would make for a festival-winning film. Jen finally succumbed to a brief nap in the waiting room, drained of all energy. She dreamt of days passed—her graduations, her wedding day, Jason's birth. Then, suddenly the pleasant scenes crumbled to a black dust, replaced by the darkness of Jason's abduction, the whirling snowstorm and Jeffrey's operation. She gasped with terror as she awoke, afraid that she might have missed any important detail. Slowly, Jen found her way to the phone and called Jason.

"Yes, he's okay now. No, I didn't want to alarm you. He needed an operation, but he came through it all right. I'm waiting for him to come around from the anesthesia. I'm sorry you had to wait so long to hear from me. Did you eat something? Go ahead and go to sleep. I'll call you when I have more news on dad. I love you, hon," Jen let the phone slip through her fingers, back into the cradle.

Still exhausted, she thumbed through the magazines in the waiting room aimlessly. Nothing interested her until she noticed the healthcare magazine with the doctors on the cover. Four doctors in surgical garb stood smiling. She could have sworn one of them was Dr. Mustafa. She dismissed the thought, writing it off to her current lack of mental clarity. Finally, she approached the nurse's station. No one in sight. She waited. An older nurse ambled over, glancing across the top of her glasses inquisitively at Jen.

"Could you please find out if my husband is out of recovery yet. His name is Jeffrey Clyman," Jen announced.

"Clyman, Clyman; let me see. Ah, that's Dr. Francis's patient, right?"

"Yes, yes. He just operated on him this evening," Jen felt so strange saying the words.

Nurse Gladys picked up her phone and began punching buttons calmly as she tapped her pen on the clipboard in front of her.

"Hmm. Nobody's answering down there. Let me go and have a look, my dear," she smiled at Jen.

Again, Jen became obsessed as she watched the hands on the wall clock laboriously turn. Finally, nurse Gladys returned and escorted Jen back down the long corridor to the recovery room. Just then, an Asian nurse and a Black nurse's aide emerged, wheeling Jeffrey out. Jen's heart raced as he opened his eyes and reached his hand out to her.

"You didn't think I would miss my welcome party now, did you?" Jeffrey winked at her.

They followed the nurse and the aide into a dark, empty room. Once situated, they began to hook up the tubes and wires to monitor Jeffrey's condition. A figure appeared at the door.

"I'll take it from here," the familiar accent struck their ears.

Dr. Mustafa entered the room, wearing his customary white lab coat. The nurse and the aide promptly left.

"You had a close call, Mr. Clyman. But it appears you did not need my help. You pulled through on your own. Miracles do happen," he smiled at Jen and quickly left the room.

Jen masked her confusion, not wanting to alarm Jeffrey.

"So, you think their cooking is any where as good as yours?" Jeffrey joked.

Jen breathed a sigh of relief at his mood.

"I guess we're going to find out soon, aren't we?" Jen mused.

Home after a week in the hospital, Jeffrey began to feel his strength return gradually. As much as he missed the stimulation of the law practice, he noticed himself feeling a sense of relief for the first time away from the office. He wondered what John Calendar and his cohorts would undertake next. An uneasiness set in whenever he thought about the close call with Jason's youthful abduction ten years ago. It annoyed him that he felt so powerless. Still, he did all he could to suppress any outward indication of these feelings to avoid upsetting Jen—and especially not to set Jason off. More than once, they had to deal with the scarring trauma left in the wake of the incident. A special needs child like Jason typically had less resilience to recover from an experience like this. While he was home recovering, Jeffrey took careful note of his son's demeanor. He sensed an undercurrent and discussed it with Jen, discreetly.

"What do you think about bringing Jason back to your old friend, Dr. Sharah? Do you think she could help?" Jeffrey leaned over to Jen just before she drifted off to sleep.

"I'll call her tomorrow. Good suggestion. You always come up with the right ideas," Jen kissed Jeffrey on the forehead, then buried her head under the sheet.

Jason reluctantly agreed to see Dr. Sharah later that week.

"I remember you, ma'am. Only you look older now," Jason nodded to Dr. Sharah.

"And so do you, Jason," she teased.

"I didn't want to come today. I did it because mom asked me to," Jason confided.

"And why is that—that you didn't want to come here today?" Dr. Sharah placed her hand on Jason's shoulder, taking care to stand at arm's length and give him space.

"I guess I don't want to remember things sometimes. Bad things," Jason shifted his weight from one leg to the other.

"Jason, you know this is a safe space, don't you? That nothing can harm you here. You know that, right?" Dr. Sharah sought to reassure him.

"Yeah. I guess so," Jason lowered his eyes to the floor.

"Do you still have your cats?" Jason smiled.

"No, they're gone now. So, let me tell you what I would like to do today, Jason," Dr. Sharah probed for his acceptance.

"Okay, go ahead," Jason slumped into a chair.

"I'm going to close the curtains, darken the room, light just this one candle and I'm going to ask you to take me with you on a journey inside your mind. We're going to explore together, all right?" Dr. Sharah leaned forward, taking both of Jason's hands in her own and looked directly into his eyes.

"Okay, but can we stop if it hurts?" Jason implored.

"Sometimes hurting is important. We need to be willing to experience all feelings," Dr. Sharah sat back in her chair.

"Now, close your eyes and take a deep breath. You're in your room at home. You're ten years old. It's a stormy night and you hear noises outside. Now you hear voices. The voices are coming closer. Now they're in your room. What happens next?" Dr. Sharah queried.

"The two men have raincoats and hats—the kind old-time detectives used to wear. One of them leans over me and puts his hand over my mouth. He tells me not to talk and everything will be all right. The other one tells me to get dressed. They wait for me. I follow them out the back door. They tell me to get into a car. We drive away. They tell me not to look back, and not to tell anyone anything that happens after this. I'm scared," Jason's voice quivered.

"All right; you're doing fine, Jason. Just keep up the good work.Tell me everything you remember. Use all of your senses. Tell me what you see, what you hear, what you smell," Dr. Sharah probed gently.

"We go to that big house where my dad's boss lives. They take me down a hallway and into an office room. Then I follow them into a secret passage behind a wall full of books. It's cloudy and foggy. I can't see anything but blue light. Then, we get into a different car—an old one, and the two men drive again. It's still dark, so I don't see too much. Then, I recognize the highway and I see lights and signs. We go to the airport, but it looks different. There's only a few buildings and they don't look modern like I remember them. They stop the car in front of a building and take me inside. It's a gigantic empty building—like a place where you would keep a plane. It smells like a basement.

I look around. They tell me to sit with a group of other kids. I can tell that they are different, these kids—like me. They can do things, see things, feel things other people can't. I somehow just know it. We're at one end of the building, and at the other end, there's a group of grown-ups sitting at a long table. In the middle of the room, there are two groups of people. On one side, there are sick people; on the other side, there are bad people with chains. Two of the men from the long table get up. They point to us one by one and tell us to stand between the two groups of people. I don't want to go. I'm scared. We're all scared. But they tell us if we want to ever go home again, we have to come. So, we get up and stand between the two tables. I feel a little sick. Then the two men from the long table start to wave their hands over the bad people in chains. Then I see the blue light and a hear a whirring sound. Now they wave their arms over the sick people. The bad people are choking and can't breathe. The sick people sit up. Now they want us to do it to the next person at the table. I won't do it. I yell out, 'you're killing them. I won't kill them.' I want to run, but I'm too scared. The other kids start to do it, but I won't. I want to cover my eyes, but they won't let me. It feels like someone took all the air out of the room; it's hard to breathe.

Then the two men from the long table tell the two men that brought me there to take me to another room. We go into a small room with glass windows. I can still see the other kids doing it. I feel really sick. They offer me food, but I don't want to eat. I fall asleep after a while. When I wake up, I feel a little better, but I'm still scared. I look through the window, but all the kids are gone. The people at the long table, too. And the sick people; and the bad people. Everybody is gone. They leave me alone for a long time. I try the door, but it's locked. I bang on the window, but nobody comes. I shout loud, but nobody answers. I start pacing the floor. Now I'm hungry. After a long time, the two men that brought me there come back with a paper bag and offer me a sandwich and a bottle of soda. At first, I'm afraid maybe they put something bad in the food, but then I start to eat.

Finally, they tell me to follow them. They drive me back to my house, but it looks different—and other people are living there. I start to cry. I tell them I want to see my mother and father. They take me back to their old car and we drive back to the big house on the hill. We go inside. They tell me to sit in a big chair in the office room. My dad's boss comes in, but he looks younger. He starts walking around my chair and looks down at me. Then he talks to me."

"Jason, we chose you for a very important assignment, but unfortunately, you did not pass the test. You see, all of the children you saw have special abilities like you. We are doing something very important to keep the world safe. You had the chance to help us, but *you* decided not to. It was *your* choice, not ours. You must never tell anyone what you saw. It must remain a secret. Now, I know you want to go home. Can you keep a secret?" John Calendar implored.

"Yes," Jason nodded, swallowing hard.

"All right then. These two men will take you home. Just follow them as you did before," John Calendar instructed Jason.

"I followed the two men behind the wall of books again. The foggy blue light surrounded us. I could not see anything. When it got clear again, they lead me outside to the car they used when they first came to my house. Nobody said a word. They drove me back home. I was afraid the other people would be there when I got to my house. I opened the door and my parents hugged me. That's all I remember," Jason breathed heavily.

"You did great, Jason. I'm very proud of you, "Dr. Sharah nodded, placing a hand on Jason's shoulder.

"Now, that's the first time you ever told anybody anything about this experience in ten years, Jason. Do you feel better, now that you've told somebody what happened to you?"

"Yes, Dr. Sharah."

"Jason, do you have any idea what this all means?" Dr. Sharah leaned in, looking Jason directly in the eye.

"No ma'am. It just seemed like a bad dream to me. I don't understand why anyone would do what these people did, and why they wanted us kids to do it, too," Jason looked confused.

"Perhaps it was like a bad dream—nothing for you to worry about, "Dr. Sharah consoled Jason as she breathed on her eyeglasses and then wiped them on her scarf.

"Just like a bad dream. That's all," Dr. Sharah repeated.

Chapter V

2006

The alarm went off. Jeffrey rolled over and turned it off. He looked around with a start. Jen had already arisen. He lacked the energy he once had—not to mention the enthusiasm for his work. He stumbled out of bed and made his way into the bathroom, which began to show signs of aging. The peeling paint reminded him of his own complexion—ruddy and pasty. Jeffrey seldom drank, yet his eyes looked bloodshot. Too many late evenings poring over documents; too many long hours staring at a computer screen. He splashed the cold water on his face. It stung his eyes; they blurred, then slowly cleared. He refocused, glancing across the hallway at Jen, hunched over their home computer. Jeffrey ambled over, planting a kiss on her forehead. The morning sun made her hair glisten—not the way it once did. Now, the silver-gray strands reflected back. He studied her face as she leaned back into his chest. Only a few fine lines graced her visage. He ran his hand along her neck, tracing the outline with his fingers, gently.

"Feel like going back to bed?" he teased, playfully.

"Never mind what I feel like. You've got a desk full of work waiting for you at your office, I'm sure," she poked his slightly protruding belly.

"There's always tonight, doctor," he smiled back, withdrawing from the room.

"If you're *up to it*, counselor," she stared at his crotch and winked at him.

Jeffrey suited up and pulled the car out of the garage in a hurry, noticing the time. He didn't even stop for his usual breakfast on the go. His mind began to wander. He seemed to slip back in time, recalling his first encounter with the soul switchers, Jason's birth, Jason's abduction, all as he drove. He nearly collided with a truck as he snapped back to the present, realizing at the last minute that the traffic light had turned red. He jerked the wheel; the truck driver leaned on his horn; Jeffrey felt his heart race.

Much had changed at the Calendar law firm. The new receptionist flashed a smile as Jeffrey waved to her. She reminded him so much of Jen in her younger days. Young associates buzzed about, laptop computers under their arms. Jeffrey mused over the number of folders they would have had to carry back in the day. The old guard had all but disappeared—died off, retired out or just moved on to new firms. The weeding out process never seemed to stop. Still, the firm marched on, remaining a powerhouse in the legal community. John Calendar's overarching presence and influence kept it moving, like the gears in an old clock that continued to tick and tick and—Jeffrey nearly bumped into the young paralegal that brushed by him. He caught the scent of her fragrance wafting past him—another reminder of his younger days.

Jeffrey opened his office door, pulled open the blinds and settled into the chair. He fired up the desk top computer. One message, from John Calendar himself. Jeffrey had long since stopped worrying about his future—at the firm, or in this life. The firm had provided him with a comfortable enough lifestyle for his family. That seemed all that mattered to a sixty-five-year-old. Jeffrey had even begun to entertain the thought of retiring. It seemed to loom closer than ever on this particular day. He no longer felt obligated to John Calendar. He had paid his dues. He had even ceased to worry about the soul switchers. They would accomplish their mission—whatever it was—with or without him.

Jeffrey knocked on John Calendar's office door, which stood ajar. John Calendar motioned him to come in. Jeffrey pointed to the door, as if to ask whether Mr. Calendar wanted it open or shut. John Calendar assumed his usual pose—standing poised behind the desk, silhouetted against the window in the morning sun. Jeffrey sat back and waited.

"Clyman, I give this speech to all of my senior associates, so I'm not singling you out. You know that I've never made *anybody* here a partner, don't you? Well, that may change.What are your thoughts on taking on that role?" John Calendar held Jeffrey's gaze.

"Sir, I was actually thinking about *retiring* soon, in all honesty," Jeffrey responded cautiously.

"Not in this lifetime, Clyman. I need you here. Somebody's got to teach these young bucks how we work here. Besides, I'm sure you still need the money. And we have a higher purpose to accomplish, which you know about. We're going to need you to help out with that, too. We understand each other, right?" John Calendar queried emphatically.

Jeffrey nodded and headed back to his office. Nobody ever argues with John Calendar because they would never win. Now that the subject of the soul switchers came up again, Jeffrey felt trapped. John Calendar had told him a long time ago that their purpose would be revealed to him in good time. It appeared that time had come. But what would they expect him to do? He would just have to wait to find out.

That evening, Jeffrey and Jen seemed to fulfill a promise to one another—to rekindle that smoldering flame they shared. Jeffrey entered the house with a bouquet of long stem roses. The air smelled of pot pourri; candles burned on a beautifully set table and Jen lay perched on the couch like a cougar, ready to purr in her flowing satin robe. She beckoned him to the table. He followed. She dangled a strawberry over his head, snatched it away, bit into it and then ran it across his lips. Life doesn't get any sweeter than that.

Jen had prepared a superb dinner, surpassed only by an intimate, passionate session of love making that eclipsed any dessert. With an almost reckless spirit, they found themselves on the living room floor, by the fireplace. Years had passed since that kind of electricity flowed between them. They decided to settle in for the night—not to sleep, but to share and enjoy the mellow after glow.

"Jason called today. He's doing his best to adjust to the other residents at the halfway house. I'm glad he's making the effort, and not resisting. He said he has a few friends there, he's okay with the staff—and get this...he may even have a girlfriend," Jen related, smiling.

Jeffrey lay back, his arms folded behind his head on the pillow.

"Lord knows, he's been through enough. I just hope this arrangement works out. Who knows, maybe he will live independently some day," Jeffrey drew a long sigh.

"I've been thinking lately—"

"That's dangerous..."

"Seriously. I've thought about going back into practice, maybe part-time. I spoke to Dr. Sharah. She's open to having me join her practice. Of course, I would have to bring in my own patients," Jen tested out the idea on Jason.

"It's worth exploring," Jeffrey went into his lawyer mode.

"So, you're okay with the idea?" Jen braced her chin on her elbow.

"Sure, sure. Give it a try. Just make sure you and Dr. Sharah both have a clear understanding of terms. I wouldn't rule out a formal agreement," Jeffrey cautioned.

"Roger, that, counselor," Jen chuckled.

Sleep soon overcame them.

A sharp morning sun lit up the room. Jeffrey pulled the blanket over Jen and himself. A loud ring on the bedside phone alarmed them both. Jeffrey dove for the phone.

"Mr. Clyman? It's Fernanda from the halfway house. I'm sorry to bother you, but we've got a real problem. It's Jason. He flew into a rage this morning. We don't know what provoked him. He's never done this before. He threw one of my aides against the wall—picked her up over his head and tossed her. We really need you to come down here and see if you can calm him down," the excited voice blurted out, breathlessly.

"Did he hurt her? Does your staff member need medical attention? Did you have to medicate Jason?" Jeffrey tried to remain calm as Jen anxiously craned her neck to listen.

"No, don't worry. We just need him to see you and Dr. Clyman. How soon can you get down here?" Fernanda nervously queried.

"We'll get there as soon as we can—probably not more than twenty minutes," Jeffrey assured her.

He quickly explained the situation to Jen as they dressed and drove to the next town. Fair Oaks had a long reputation for easing the burden on families with special needs. Jeffrey and Jen cut through the fog, pulling into the parking lot of the imposing structure. Once inside, the front desk receptionist led them to the counselor. Grim faced, Dr. June Cavanagh arose from her desk, removing her glasses and shaking her head. She looked as though all her energy had left her body. She approached Jeffrey and Jen, motioning for them to sit down.

"I know Jason's history. I'm aware he had a traumatic incident—something difficult enough for anyone, and especially difficult for a special needs adult. He's really done fine here up until this morning. He's not talking to us, so we still don't know why he snapped. We had hoped maybe you can get him to open up," Dr. Cavanagh implored them.

"We'll try our best. Please just take us to him," Jen looked hopeful.

Dr. Cavanagh led them down a long corridor, passing the residents' rooms. A few young adults peered out at them curiously. Jeffrey wrapped his arm around Jen in a protective gesture. They felt an undercurrent of hostility as they whisked by. Finally, they entered a large room with high, vaulted ceilings, bathed in incandescent light from the large overhead fixtures. Jason sat on the floor in the corner, his back against the wall, like a wounded animal in a cage. Jeffrey and Jen removed their coats and sat on the floor in front of him. He began rocking back and forth, slowly at first, then more rapidly. He muttered and began to slam his back against the wall. Jeffrey quickly dropped his coat behind Jason to cushion the impact.

"Jason, we're here for you. Tell us how we can help you," Jen held both of his hands in her own and looked into Jason's eyes.

"They came again. They tried to take me again. I did not go this time. I did not go. I told them to leave, and they did. They still want me to do it, but I won't. I won't ever do it," Jason's voice became gruff and agitated.

"If they left, then why did you hurt that girl?" Jen gently smoothed his hair back from his profusely perspiring forehead.

"She was one of them. She wanted me to go with them. I will not go. I will not go—ever again. I had to keep them away," Jason became breathless and slid down, limply.

"You never have to go, but you can't hurt the people who are here to help you," Jen leaned over to console him.

"You can go now. I will be all right. I'm glad you came," Jason slowly arose, calmly nodding his head as if he had awakened from a bad dream.

Jeffrey and Jen left quietly. On the ride home, they couldn't help but wonder if the soul switchers had actually tried to take Jason, or if he had experienced a flashback of sorts from his earlier trauma. Even with all of her training, Jen could only speculate. She wondered whether he should see Dr. Sharah again. Jeffrey disagreed.

"You are already too close to the situation, as a family member. Now that you are going into practice with Dr. Sharah, as your partner, that also makes her too close, " Jeffrey intoned, his voice cracking.

"Let's see how it plays out," Jen sighed, leaning her head against Jeffrey's shoulder as he turned the corner.

Still, something didn't seem right to either one of them. The uneasiness gnawed at both of them. They simply could not dismiss their concern over Jason's state of mind—and over the soul switchers' encroachment on their lives. A wind blew the leaves from the sidewalk against their windshield, nearly obscuring their view. Jeffrey blinked, refocused and activated the windshield wipers in an effort to clear the leaves away. A light rain punctuated the scene. More leaves swirled. The streetlights came on. Home at last.

Jen embarked on the necessary preparations for her new practice. From partnership agreements to freshening up her wardrobe, to business cards and announcements, she quickly moved in to the shared office space with Dr. Sharah. It felt right, at least at first. Then one morning Jen ran to answer the ringing office phone and collided with Dr. Sharah, spilling coffee all over her. Dr. Sharah always wore those long dresses with a flowing cape over them. Jen froze, then furiously tried to wipe Dr. Sharah's cape dry.

"No worries, my dear; no worries," Dr. Sharah cooed, removing the cape and rolling up the wet sleeve of her dress.

Jen stopped, trying to conceal her surprise. She could not help but notice the two intertwined "S" marks on Dr. Sharah's arm. Dr. Sharah smiled.

"No worries," she repeated.

"Sit, darling. Let's talk. So, how much do you know about our mission?" Dr. Sharah probed, fixing her gaze on Jen.

"Not very much, really. We've known about you people for a long time, but we have very little knowledge of the program," Jen responded candidly, sipping her coffee.

"Well, do you have an opinion about our mission? Surely, you must know something of what we have planned," Dr. Sharah remained fixed on Jen's eyes.

"They've told us very little, like I said. What little we know, we found out by accident," Jen avoided displaying any emotion.

"Well, the program has affected you close to home, so you must have some feeling about it," Dr. Sharah queried.

Jen felt her colleague trying to manipulate her into a corner. She resisted the urge to react.

"Honestly, we know what your people are capable of; we really don't know why they're doing it," Jen did her best to continue masking her feelings about Jason's abduction.

"Well, I'm really not supposed to tell you, but we genuinely seek to make the world a better place. Doesn't everyone want that?" Dr. Sharah leaned in and placed her hand on Jen's shoulder.

Another manipulation. Jen didn't answer.

"You want to know why we recruited the children. I understand completely. You see, even though we can time travel, our bodies still age. We need to train the next generation to continue carrying on our vital work. There's nothing nefarious about it, I assure you," Dr. Sharah leaned back on the couch and stretched out her arms.

"Then, why my son?" Jen suddenly snapped.

"I knew you would ask that question. We all know Jason has special abilities. We simply thought they might help him perform the task more effectively. All of the children we selected had special talents," Dr. Sharah smiled—as if she had made some holy pronouncement.

"So, where do we go from here?" Jen confronted her coldly.

"Why, we move forward in building our practice, my dear. Why should this change anything? Your husband works among our people," Dr. Sharah added.

Jen felt a twinge in the pit of her stomach. She had the sudden urge to run, but she knew she had to do exactly the opposite. She stood her ground.

"And I suppose we will dedicate our practice to 'making the world a better place' ", Jen arose from her chair and left Dr. Sharah sitting alone. After half an hour, Jen's head began to burst with thoughts of betrayal. She began to wonder what schemes Dr. Sharah had participated in. Events had come full circle—and landed right back in Jen's lap. This hit too close to home. She began to seethe in a way she had never done before. Her mothering instinct took full control. Without warning, she sat squarely in front of Dr. Sharah, took hold of both of her hands and stared into her eyes. Jen pointed to the two serpentine marks on Dr. Shara's arms.

"Now, we're going to have a conversation—and I need the truth," she nearly spit the words out, venomously.

Dr. Sharah remained calm, unfazed.

Jen continued, on the attack.

"Did you, or did you not know about my son's abduction *before* it happened?"

Dr. Sharah smiled, jerked her hand free and removed her glasses, returning Jen's stare.

"I know many things. Some I will share with you and some I can't—

"Or maybe just won't," Jen interrupted, still seething.

Jen leaned in, nearly nose to nose with Dr. Sharah.

"I'll ask you one more time, and only one more—and this time, I need the truth. Did you know about my son's abduction before it happened?"

Dr. Sharah lightly pushed Jen back a safe distance and shook her head, sighing.

"So many questions, so few answers. Yes, I did know—but I couldn't stop it if I wanted to," Dr. Sharah nearly laughed her response, which irritated Jen even more.

"All right. Let's continue. Were you in any way *involved* in my son's abduction?" Jen pressed on.

"That depends on what you mean by *involved*," Dr. Sharah seemed to smirk back at Jen.

"Did you knowingly order or participate in any of what occurred?" Jen gritted her teeth at Dr. Sharah.

"No, I did not," Dr. Sharah let out a sigh, as if her answer somehow vindicated her.

"Have you ever gone through any of the portals yourself?" Jen queried, backing down slightly.

"No, no, my dear. I'm afraid that's as they say, 'above my pay grade,' Dr. Sharah replied.

"But surely you know what effects it has—time traveling through these portals. You said the experiment came about because the soul switchers needed to replace their ranks with younger people—that their bodies age, even though they travel through time. What happens when they time travel?" Jen slowly arose, standing over Dr. Sharah.

"Well, we have run some tests, but we don't have definitive results—"

"What effect does time travel through the portals have on a person's body?" Jen cut her off.

"There are some molecular anomalies resulting...possibly some DNA scrambling, premature aging, maybe hormonal imbalances in a few rare cases," Dr. Sharah responded in her dry clinician's voice.

Jen once again went on the attack, now furious.

"You people took the chance of permanently altering the lives of innocent young people to perpetuate your political and social agenda? And even put vulnerable special needs children at greater risk? What is wrong with you people? You do realize we could have prosecuted people for this," Jen shouted at Dr. Sharah.

"Very doubtful. We reach up to some very high places. And besides, you know how much good we've done for this country—and will soon do for the whole planet, ridding it of the scourge, those who don't deserve to live—they who have squandered the gift of life," Dr. Sharah spouted out the same platitudes Jeffrey had heard from the likes of John Calendar and his circle of influence.

Jen turned her back, gathered up her briefcase and purse and stormed out the door.

When she arrived home, Jen confronted Jeffrey with the events of her day. He did not appear shocked, but visibly distraught.

"I'm guessing you have something equally upsetting to share with me," she could read the worry lines on his face.

"I left the firm today. Just up and quit. But not until I overheard John Calendar reporting his latest victories. They racked up over a thousand switched souls in one night. This thing has spread from coast to coast. It reaches up to the highest levels in government. Jen, we've got to get out of here!" Jeffrey nearly shouted at her.

"Where can we go that they wouldn't find us?" Jen followed him into the bedroom.

"Just get in the car now. We're picking Jason up. I'll tell you on the way. I've got a plan that will have their heads spinning," Jeffrey threw a few items of clothing into a bag.

In minutes, they careened around the corner, raced to beat every traffic light and pulled up to Jason's halfway house. Jen kept the motor running while Jeffrey bounded up the front steps. Out of breath, he blew past the front desk, up the stairway and slid into Jason's room, startling him.

"Dad, what's going on? Where's mom?" Jason peered around the doorway.

"Grab your jacket and follow me. Don't say a word to anyone. Just keep moving," Jeffrey ushered him down the back stair well and around the building.

"Get in the car. I'll explain later. We've got to go," Jeffrey dropped into the driver's seat as Jason slumped down in the back.

"Dad, are you okay? Mom, what's up with him?" Jason leaned forward between the seats.

In a few minutes, Jeffrey arrived at the Calendar mansion. Darkness had begun to fall. He knew he had to get inside before John Calendar returned home. With Jen and Jason in tow, he knocked briskly on the front door. The butler opened it. Surprised to see Jeffrey, he backed away, sensing danger. Jeffrey reached out, grabbed his necktie and pushed past him.

"We're going to the study. I know where it is. You're going to tell me how to operate the portal," Jeffrey growled at the frightened man servant.

After a quick walk down the hall, they entered the darkened study. Jeffrey approached the bookcase. Feeling around, he located the hidden access button. The door opened. The blue fog enveloped them as they entered. One after another, they stepped forward and felt themselves sucked through the portal. None of them knew where they would end up. They just knew they had to leave.

Chapter VI

1946

The blue fog that enveloped the Clyman family gradually dissipated. Jeffrey held Jen and Jason tightly against him, breathing deeply.

"Are you okay?" he asked each of them.

"Yeah. Just a little lightheaded," Jen blinked her eyes.

"You, Jason?"

"I guess the same. I remember that feeling. I had that when they took me. Where are we, dad?" Jason looked puzzled.

"The same place we were—just a different time. It does feel weird. I have this strange bodily sensation, like I can feel all the cells inside of me moving around," Jeffrey mopped his brow with his sleeve.

"Hey dad, look at that old car in front of the house!" Jason exclaimed.

"That gives me a clue at least, of approximately the year. It looks like a 1940's model. Stay here. I'm going to take a peek at that newspaper on the front lawn," Jeffrey jogged over, picking up the rolled-up newspaper.

"1946. It's 1946. Well, well. If we only knew how to control this time travel. Let's see what we can learn," Jeffrey walked briskly towards Jen and Jason.

"Hey, mister. You trying to steal our paper? My dad wouldn't like that," they turned around to see a teenage boy with a baseball bat and glove staring at them from the front steps.

"Not at all, son. Our car broke down outside of town last night. We had a long walk and we're just waiting to find out how long it will take to repair. What's your name?" Jeffrey queried.

"John Calendar. I live here with my dad. Mom's dead. Died in a hurricane, visiting her family," the boy replied.

"Well, you sound like a smart young man, Mr. Calendar. I'll bet your dad is a real upstanding man himself," Jeffrey responded.

"He's a professor and a famous physicist. His name is Dr. Julius Calendar. Have you heard of him?" John asked, heading toward the house.

"Yes, I believe I have, son. He's a brilliant man," Jeffrey nodded and waved goodbye.

Young John Calendar disappeared from view, behind the house. A moment later the Clyman trio heard the sound of glass breaking, followed by a man shouting out the back door.

"John Calendar, to the woodshed! I've told you a hundred times not to play ball that close to the house," the muffled voice rang out.

"You know the drill. Drop your drawers. Do it, now! And your shorts. Quickly, or I'll do it for you," the voice barked.

Dr. Calendar entered the dark space of the woodshed, officiously removing his jacket and rolling up his sleeves as though he were about to perform an operation. Swiftly, he withdrew his belt, raised his arm and brought it down with a full force strike.

The Clymans heard the sound of the leather searing young John Calendar's flesh repeatedly.

"Oww! Please, no more, dad, please; enough."

"I'll decide when you've had enough."

The cries subsided to sobbing.

"Go ahead and bawl like a baby. You'll just get more of the same," the voice rang out.

"He's really mean," Jason whispered to Jeffrey.

Jeffrey caught himself, realizing that he began to enjoy young John Calendar's punishment. Then he came to realize what shaped the man he knew later in life as his boss—seemingly fearless and unfeeling. Jeffrey began to conceive a plan to learn what they needed to know. They approached the front door. Jeffrey grabbed the brass knocker and firmly rapped on the door three times. An officious looking butler cautiously opened the door.

"Yes?" he inquired.

"My wife, my son and I are admirers of Dr. Calendar's. I'm an attorney at law myself, but I've always loved the work of scientists and inventors. We wondered if we might meet your esteemed employer?" Jeffrey poured it on thick.

"I'll see if he's in and if he cares to receive guests," the butler answered, curtly.

After a long wait in the foyer, the butler returned and motioned for the Clymans to follow him down the long corridor to the study. It looked nearly the same as it did all those years later. The butler closed the door behind them as Dr. Calendar stood up and strode forward to greet them.

"So, I understand you are admirers of my work. And how, pray tell, did you hear of it?" Dr. Calendar's ego began to inflate.

"Oh, I read scientific journals whenever I get the chance. And I encourage my son to read them, as well. My wife prefers lighter reading, of course," Jeffrey smiled as Dr. Calendar adjusted his spectacles.

"And you want to know about my latest experiments, I take it, Mr.—what did you say your name was?" Dr. Calendar smiled back at Jeffrey.

"Clyman, Jeffrey Clyman, sir. Yes, we would love to hear all about your new conquests. Would it be space or time?" Jeffrey knew he had the professor hooked.

"Both, Mr. Clyman. Neither space nor time can exist or move without the other. If you travel through space, you will also travel through time. If you travel through time, however, the relationship to space will change. While it may appear that you have not moved, you in fact have done so. Allow me to demonstrate," Dr. Calendar picked up the pen from his desk and flung it across the room, narrowly missing Jason's head.

"The amount of time it takes to move through space is inversely proportional to the amount of space required to move through time. Do you understand?" Dr. Calendar peered over the top of his glasses at each of the Clyman family members.

"So, do you think that in our lifetimes we will be able to conquer both space and time?" Jeffrey challenged him.

"Of course we will. I'm working on it as we speak. In fact, I have a dedicated team performing experiments on it now. We have nearly perfected a machine to accelerate the process. Perhaps when it is ready,

I can show it to you. Would you like to see that?" Dr. Calendar's eyes sparkled.

"Why, yes, sir. We most certainly would. When do you think it will be ready?" Jeffrey prodded.

"You are in luck. This very night we will gather to test it, right here," Dr. Calendar rubbed his hands together. He had the air of a magician, ready to reveal his greatest trick.

"Then consider yourselves invited. Eight o'clock sharp," Dr. Calendar arose from his chair and led them to the door.

Jeffrey had led him to exactly where he wanted the man.

The Clymans exited the Calendar mansion, smiling. They looked back toward the house in time to see a red-faced young John Calendar peering out a second-floor window at them. Jeffrey couldn't help but revel over the thought that he had achieved an advantage over John Calendar. They began walking down the road. Once out of view of the Calendar home, Jeffrey, Jen and Jason huddled together. A Westfield Police car whizzed past them, siren blaring and light flashing.

"We can walk to the park from here. Let's lay low until this evening. We'll return to the Calendar home and see what we can learn from this 'demonstration'," Jeffrey offered.

The park hadn't changed much in all those years either. The large pond reflected the sunlight. Bicyclists rode past them; ducks flew overhead. After an hour, hunger began to overtake the Clyman family. Once again, Jeffrey had to use his best cunning to manifest a meal for the family. They walked down Broad Street to the five-and-ten store. Jeffrey entered first, asking for the manager.

"I'm an attorney-at-law and just as a friendly gesture, I want to let you know that the town council recently passed a new ordinance. If you don't repair those cracks in the sidewalk out front, they are going to fine you. The town might even shut down your store. I would hate to see that happen to you. You have so many people that love to shop here," Jeffrey nodded.

The manager went pale, thanked Jeffrey profusely, then offered to buy him and his family a meal. At first Jeffrey refused, insisting he wanted nothing in return for his information. The more he declined, the more the manager begged him to sit down. The plan worked. The Clymans read the menu on the wall of the luncheonette counter, marveling at the prices. Ten cents for a soda; fifty cents for a grilled cheese sandwich! They devoured the meal and left quietly, returning to the park.

As night fell, the Clymans made the trek back up Mountain Avenue and on to Hillside Avenue, approaching the Calendar mansion. Cars began pulling up the long driveway. Jeffrey guessed that Professor Clyman's team of scientists made up the contingent. They waited until the last man entered before approaching the door.

This time, no officious butler greeting—a nod and they were ushered down the hall and into the familiar Calendar estate great room, where the other attendees assembled. Jeffrey, of course, knew the lay of the land and did not exhibit the slightest bit of nervousness. Trays of champagne glasses made their way around the room. Jeffrey, Jen and Jason scanned the crowd as Dr. Calendar began the introductions: Senator McCord, Governor Whiteside, Dr. Cohn, Dr. Friedrich. He paused when he motioned toward the Clymans. Jeffrey spoke up.

"Jeffrey Clyman, attorney-at-law, and my wife and son; very pleased to witness this groundbreaking event," Jeffrey's voice rang out, echoing off of the mahogany paneled room.

Just then, Jeffrey caught a glimpse of young John Calendar peeking through the crack in the doorway and then disappearing quickly.

"Gentlemen—and lady, let us proceed to the library, where the demonstration will begin shortly," Dr. Calendar lead the group down the hall and into the dimly lit study.

Jeffrey put his arms around Jen and Jason, carefully studying Dr. Calendar's every move. He wanted to know everything he could about the project. Dr. Calendar released the hidden lever in the bookcase, revealing a stainless-steel archway. His university colleagues Dr. Cohn and Dr. Friedrich rolled a metal cart forward. A machine full of vacuum tubes and wires sat on top of the cart. Jeffrey observed as they plugged the machine in to a wall outlet and began to turn the crank on a magneto. Sparks flew; the tubes lit up; the Senator and the Governor murmured. Dr. Calendar stepped forward and began to speak again.

"I give you Project Chronos. Yes, we have conquered the secret of time. My colleagues and I have, after much research, isolated a method to disrupt and capture the space-time continuum, allowing time travel.

We have tested, re-tested and improved the experience after numerous trials. Please observe, as my colleagues bring forth a subject," Dr. Calendar extolled the virtues of his work.

Dr. Cohn placed a caged rabbit under the steel archway as Dr. Friedrich continued to crank the magneto. The familiar whirring sound gradually increased in intensity; the blue light began to envelop the archway. A fog clouded the frightened, caged rabbit. Its lips quivered. In a moment, the whirring wound down to an inaudible pitch; the blue fog dissipated; and the stunned onlookers stared at an empty cage.

"This is no parlor trick, I assure you," Dr. Calendar strode forward, beckoning the attendees to assemble in the chairs surrounding his desk.

"What use, exactly, do you intend to make of this 'discovery?'" Senator McCord inquired, adjusting his bow tie.

"Sir, we just concluded one war overseas; now, we have another to fight here at home. We quelled the Nazi juggernaut; we have yet to tame the Communist beast. Do you not see the value of such a discovery?" Dr. Calendar leaned forward, his arms outstretched on his desk.

Governor Whiteside lit a cigar, blew a smoke ring and began to laugh.

"Indeed, I do, and I'm sure our esteemed, patriotic Senator does as well, don't you Cyrus?"

Senator McCord leaned forward in his chair, addressing Dr. Calendar directly:

"That depends upon who is in control of Project Chronos. We can't just have any fool hopping and skipping along through time whenever he feels like it. Besides the obvious, are there any other benefits to this expensive toy you've built?"

Dr. Calendar raised a hand and gestured broadly, responding directly to the query:

"As a matter of fact, there are. We've just begun our human trials, and quite by accident, we became aware of a fortuitous side effect of the time travel when we followed and returned one of our animal subjects. Repeated exposure to the portal and its effects gives one the ability to transfer the life force from one being to another. Now do you find our work useful enough to continue funding it?"

Senator McCord turned to Governor Whiteside, smiling.

"I'll take this one, if you don't mind, Richard. Dr. Calendar, we'll consider extending your grant for another year—with conditions, of course."

"What conditions are those, if I may ask?" Dr. Calendar stepped out from behind his desk.

"We're going to have to keep a tight lid on this. From here on out, based on the new information we have, Project Chronos will have Top Secret status. We will, of course, require continuous updates on the progress of your experiments. More importantly, we will have complete control over who uses this, as well as when and *how* they use it," Senator McCord arose from his chair, nodded and placed his Fedora firmly on his head.

The Senator and the Governor departed; Drs. Cohn and Friedrich replaced the equipment to its original spot, removed their lab coats and headed for the door. Jeffrey, Jen and Jason began to arise from their chairs; Dr. Calendar motioned for them to stay. Perched on the edge of his desk, he removed his glasses, polished them with his handkerchief, furrowed his brow and addressed the Clymans.

"Well, what did you think of our little show tonight?"

Jeffrey spoke up.

"Why, I'm thoroughly impressed. How could anyone not be? I would love to hear more about how the device actually works. How do you control it, for example, for precise intervals of time?"

Jeffrey could see Dr. Calendar's eyes light up.

"I will tell you what. Have dinner, stay the night as my house guests and tomorrow, I will give you a detailed explanation," Dr. Calendar offered.

"We couldn't impose on you; such a kind offer, we must decline," Jen spoke up taking a cue from Jeffrey's technique to maneuver the conversation.

"I insist. We will dine and then retire early. No, no; you must accept," Dr. Calendar implored them.

The officious butler served a modest, but well-prepared meal. Young John Calendar remained conspicuous by his absence—no doubt a continuation of his punishment for breaking the window earlier that day. Dr. Calendar monopolized the conversation, extolling the perceived virtues he gained by partnering with the government.

"You see, universities are, by nature, bureaucratic and constrained. They don't often see the big picture. We are on the verge of a new era—able to have a cataclysmic impact on the world. In all modesty, I must say, our discoveries will not only alter history—they will, in effect, *create* the future. You see, unseen forces control much of what we see, hear and ultimately believe about our world. We, the modern explorers of new worlds, must retain a stake in the execution and delivery of the grand design—the big mission, if you will," Dr. Calendar waved his wine glass in a flourish.

"Please, if you will, for our enlightenment, clarify that mission. We're not privy to it as you are," Jeffrey probed gently as the butler refilled his glass, then Jen and Jason's.

"The civilized world has a bold imperative. While it may sound altruistic to speak of protecting the inferior and impoverished races, in reality we need to remain the good stewards of our intellectual property. The fruits of our labor must not be allowed to wither, as I am sure you understand. So just what is our mission, you ask? It is nothing short of protecting the future survival of humanity. We plan to prevent overpopulation, and to reign in the evil abuses of mankind. Those who do not value life simply do not deserve to have it," Dr. Calendar slammed the table with the palm of his hand, rattling the glassware and china.

Jeffrey raised his glass, nodding.

"Well said, sir; well said. We cannot thank you enough for your gracious hospitality—and for sharing your outlook and insights. We thoroughly appreciate the opportunity to witness your discoveries and to share your views. We really must retire and let you get some rest. I'm sure you have another very important day ahead of you," Jeffrey downed the last of his wine.

"I'll have my butler show you to your rooms," Dr. Calendar arose from his chair and took a bow, as though completing a performance.

Night fell and a cool breeze swept over the picturesque, idyllic little town of Westfield. Lights began to extinguish, one by one. Birds soared; crickets chirped; insects swarmed. The mansion on Hillside Avenue loomed over its lesser neighboring structures. Well into the late hours of the night, Jeffrey awoke Jen and Jason, signaling them to follow him downstairs. The Clyman family deftly slipped into Dr.

Calendar's study. Jeffrey had carefully observed every step of the demonstration. He instructed Jason and Jen to set up the equipment exactly as he had seen Drs. Cohn and Friedrich do it. Then he began to throw the switches, turning the knobs and dials into their proper positions. As the machine began to pulsate and the whirring noise arose, he ordered Jen and Jason to stand under the archway. In seconds, he joined them. The room appeared to shake as the blue fog enveloped them. They held onto each other until they seemed to disappear.

Chapter VII

1956

Jeffrey, Jen and Jason held onto one another tightly, all of them feeling that familiar but strange bodily sensation that accompanied each and every trip through the portal. It seemed to rack their bodies more each time. Gradually, they each loosened their grip on the other, opening their eyes to a cloud covered morning. Jeffrey surveyed the scene. Evidently Dr. Calendar's theory proved correct. They found themselves down the road from the Calendar residence, not entirely sure of the day, the date or even the year. Jeffrey had hoped his careful observations of Dr. Calendar's team would afford him control over the portal. They would soon find out.

Jeffrey, Jen and Jason strolled down the road, heading for the center of town. Jason turned to Jeffrey.

"Dad, it sounds like a marching band. Listen!"

As they approached Broad Street, sure enough, they could see the parade heading for the central business district. Crowds gathered on the sidewalks flanking the street. Just then, Jen noticed a parade float approaching, preceded by the marching band. As it drew closer, they could now read the signs.

"Ike in '56."

Crowds cheered. Children hoisted on their fathers' shoulders. Leaves rained down on the crowd in the October breeze. Jeffrey reeled around. His instincts had sharpened. He motioned to Jen and Jason to keep moving.

"I think we've been followed—that black car; those two men."

The Clymans did their best to blend into the thickening crowd. The din of the marching band overpowered every voice. They passed the five and ten cent store where they had eaten ten years earlier. The two men slipped between Jeffrey and Jen.

"FBI. You need to come with us. Turn the corner ahead at Elm."

Jeffrey nodded to Jen and Jason, to follow. Once around the corner, the two men led them to the black car, opening the doors and instructing them to get in. Once inside the car, nobody spoke. In a few short moments, they knew where they were headed. The car pulled into the driveway of the Calendar residence. The FBI men opened the doors, pointing their pistols at the Clymans. No choice but to comply.

Jeffrey, Jason and Jen stood on the front steps of the Calendar mansion, the two FBI men behind them. The door opened. An older Dr. Calendar leaned on his cane, a wry smile crossing his face. He pointed his cane, indicating for them to come in.

"I've waited a long time for you. So, you stole away like thieves in the night. I suppose I'm fortunate you didn't steal my life's work. We're alone here now. My son is away at law school. Quite a surprise, don't you think? I didn't ever expect him to amount to that much. I suppose I whipped some sense into him," Dr. Calendar led them down the hallway to his study, leaning on his cane from time to time.

"Actually, you'll be quite proud of him some day. He'll make an excellent lawyer, I can assure you," Jeffrey chuckled.

"Well, you just told me what I wanted to know. So, you came here by way of my portal from the future, did you?"

Jeffrey nodded silently.

Dr. Calendar waved his cane in the direction of the FBI men.

"You can go now. I've got this under control," Dr. Calendar ordered them.

"I don't think so. They slipped through your fingers the last time. We can't afford another mistake. They know too much about the program. We're not leaving," one of the FBI men spoke for the first time.

Dr. Calendar slid down into his desk chair, one hand on his cane, the other in the top drawer. Deftly, without warning, he withdrew a small caliber pistol and brandished it at the FBI men.

"My house; my rules. Leave now, or I'll call your superiors," Dr. Calendar barked at them.

The two men turned and exited.

"Now, to the matter of my guests. You may think you know what's going on, but you really have no idea what you've stepped into here. You don't know how high this goes," Dr. Calendar peered over the top of his glasses.

"Did it cross your mind that perhaps that's why we're here—to find out?" Jeffrey leaned toward Dr. Calendar.

"Very soon, we'll elect a new President. Then we'll usher in a new era. We beat back the Nazi threat; now we need to control the spread of Communism. That ideology is the scourge of the next generation. It will tear the fabric of this country to shreds if we let it. Every manner of corruption will rule our society. Now, at last, we have the power to overcome that threat. We can give life to those who deserve it—and take it from those who place no value on it. Surely, you're civilized enough to understand the importance of this. Now, I'm going to trust you enough to leave you for a few short moments. And when I return, you will tell me just how far our experiment went," Dr Calendar raised himself from the chair with the aid of his cane.

Jason whispered to Jeffrey and Jen.

"Those two FBI men—they're the ones that took me when I was a kid. I'm sure of it," Jason appeared visibly shaken.

"Relax, son. It appears our host is just as curious about how the program progressed as we are about how it got started and who's involved," Jeffrey whispered to Jen and to Jason.

Jason, somewhat reassured, straightened up. Jeffrey and Jen saw the characteristic trance-like glaze come over him. Jason turned mechanically to face him. His voice, now steady, dropped to a monotone as he slowly pronounced the chilling words,

"He is going to die. I know it."

Dr. Calendar returned with a silver tray adorned with full silver service. Placing it on the desk, he offered Jeffrey, Jen and Jason their choice of coffee and tea.

"Let's have another go at this shall we?" Dr. Calendar suggested.

"We all have a stake in the outcome; we just need to fill in the missing pieces of the puzzle for one another. Is that fair? Don't be bashful. Please do accept my hospitality. I assure you it's not drugged," Dr. Calendar attempted to defuse the tension in the room.

"Very well, then; I'll start. As you know, we created and launched Project Chronos ten years ago with the intention and sole purpose of righting the wrongs of this world. Over the past ten years, we have penetrated government, military and police up and down the Eastern seaboard. Our movement has spread; we have grown stronger. We have only begun to unleash the power we hold. You have witnessed it yourselves. Now, tell me how far we progressed during your era," Dr. Calendar stirred his coffee with the precision of an engineer, carefully drawing out every word.

"You haven't succeeded in reaching the scale you had hoped. It's not because we stopped you. Despite your penetration into high places, Project Chronos still has not become a worldwide phenomenon. The media attention has forced your operatives to limit any measure of high-profile activity," Jeffrey responded in like manner, holding Dr. Calendar's gaze the entire time.

"And where do you think we erred in our quest?" Dr. Calendar raised his eyebrows as he took a long draught of his cooling coffee.

"Very simple; you underestimated the population. Technology moved at an extremely rapid pace in our time. As a result, people became educated and sophisticated at an equally rapid pace. They can smell a conspiracy a mile away," Jeffrey smiled broadly at Dr. Calendar.

"What civilized man and what civilized nation would not buy into what we offer? We hold in our hands the ability to create a near perfect world—not by taking life like Hitler did, but rather by giving life to those who would cherish it, appreciate it and do good with it," Dr. Calendar withdrew his pipe and began to load it with fresh tobacco.

Jeffrey's eyes never left him as he responded with poise and confidence.

"Every dictator throughout history has uttered those same words. No one has the sovereign right to exert control over others. You're playing God."

Dr. Calendar looked up from the cloud of smoke that emerged from his pipe. Furrowing his brow, he studied Jeffrey, Jason and Jen like caged animals in a zoo.

"God, you say? Surely, you jest. I am a man of ethics, but I am also a scientist. God has no place in this plan, I assure you."

Jeffrey leaned in and picked up one of the fountain pens on Dr. Calendar's desk.

"If I slit your throat with the point of this pen, what would happen to your grandiose plan? Would it march on without you?"

Dr. Calendar tapped his pipe on the ashtray. A few embers scattered across the blotter on his desk.

"Now I know you are joking. Do you really think Project Chronos would die with me? We will build more than one machine; we will harness all of the most brilliant minds this country has to offer. We will flourish," he wiped his glasses on his sweater, sinking back into his chair.

Jeffrey smiled, replacing the fountain pen in its inkwell.

"You underestimate the human spirit—and the human mind. What we learned from the horrors of war we used to shape new policies...policies that granted equality and fairness to people, regardless of their race or their gender."

"Are you aware of the proceedings in Congress known as the House Un-American Activities Committee?" Dr. Calendar queried.

"I'm not only aware of this witch hunt; I'm aware of the lives it destroyed and the bad example it set. Sorry, it may look like you will win this round, but ultimately the effort fails. I suppose your people were behind this, too?" Jeffrey confronted Dr. Calendar.

"Certainly. I told you we had a very long reach," Dr. Calendar smiled as he began to reload his pipe.

"And what happened to your friend, the Senator I met here ten years ago on our previous visit?" Jeffrey sat back in his chair.

"Poor bastard couldn't take the heat. He fell apart when he lost his bid for re-election. He took to drinking. The last I heard, he was in Muhlenberg Hospital with severe cirrhosis of the liver," Dr. Calendar let a crack of light resembling emotion peek through.

"And how is your own health?" Jeffrey probed.

"Why, it's perfectly fine. Why on earth would you even pose such a question?" Dr. Calendar's annoyance seeped through.

"No matter. Now, where were we? Oh yes, taking over the world so only the deserving would live. Did you think you would control over population? Famine? War?" Jeffrey smirked at Dr. Calendar.

"Not immediately, but eventually, yes," Dr Calendar straightened up in his chair.

Jeffrey laughed aloud.

"Then I can tell you, your experiment absolutely failed. You and your project will have had absolutely no effect on the forces controlling poverty and disease," Jeffrey counseled.

"Very well, then. In your time, just exactly what does happen to Project Chronos?" Dr. Calendar blew a cloud of smoke into the room.

"Fear. Chaos. Rebellion. That's what you and your minions have wrought. You won't stop the spread of Communism either. The larger forces of nature and economics will do that for you," Jeffrey studied Dr. Calendar for a reaction, as though he had him on a hook ready to reel him in.

Jen and Jason sat transfixed, moved by Jeffrey's resolve.

"So, I suppose you think I should just go and smash my machine and burn my notebooks, declaring Project Chronos a failure? If I did, what would become of you? You would find yourself trapped in our world and forced to play by our rules. Did you really believe it all would end here?" Dr. Calendar poured himself another cup of coffee.

"Not at all. You see, I know who will carry on your legacy—probably the last person you would suspect. But that secret will stay with me for now. By the way, how do you feel right about now?" Jeffrey queried.

Dr. Calendar scowled at him, rising out of his chair and reaching for his cane. Jeffrey snatched it away, watching the look of panic on Dr. Calendar's face as he fell forward. Jeffrey picked up the telephone on the desk, dialed the operator and calmly called for an ambulance.

Sirens blared. Lights flashed. The quiet night came alive as the ambulance crew pulled up the driveway of the Calendar mansion. The rescue squad team members grabbed a stretcher and knocked on the door. Jeffrey and Jen led them to the study, where Jason stood over Dr. Calendar's motionless body.

"Heart attack. Hope you can save him. Mind if we ride with you?" Jeffrey inquired, coolly.

"Suit yourself," the paramedic replied as they loaded Dr. Calendar onto the stretcher.

The Cadillac ambulance stopped at the emergency room entrance to Muhlenberg Hospital. Jeffrey, Jen and Jason emerged, following the ambulance crew.

Jason sat with his elbows resting on his knees. The hospital waiting room chairs lacked both comfort and style. Nurses and doctors strolled by leisurely. Jason tapped Jeffrey on the shoulder.

"Did you see that—a doctor smoking in a hospital? Is that allowed?"

"Jason, it's 1956. A lot changed from then to our time," Jeffrey smiled, patting Jason on the back.

Jen leaned her head on Jeffrey's shoulder. He stroked her hair, leaned over and whispered to her.

"I knew this would happen. You could say I *made* it happen."

Jen raised her head and turned to face Jeffrey.

"What do you mean? Are you saying you *caused* his heart attack?"

Jeffrey slid back in the chair, stretched his arms out and clasped his hands behind his neck.

"John Calendar told me his dad had a heart condition. I just gave him a push; that's all."

Jeffrey got up, leaving Jen uncomfortably surprised. He sauntered over to the nurse's station. Glancing around, he didn't see anyone. He picked up the clipboard, rifling through the pages and returned to his seat. Jen studied him, curious.

Two hours later, a nurse approached the Clyman family in the waiting area, leading them to the critical care unit where Dr. Calendar lay sleeping soundly. The oxygen tent enveloped him.

"He does look peaceful, doesn't he?" Jeffrey teased.

Jen jabbed his arm.

"What do we do now, dad?" Jason shifted from one foot to the other, studying the machines around the room.

"We wait," Jeffrey calmly assured them and led them out of the room to a small lounge at the end of the corridor.

Jeffrey left them and proceeded down the dimly lit hallway until he came to the room he had sought. Peering in, he found the sleeping Senator. His complexion had begun to exhibit the sallow tone that signified the beginnings of jaundice. In 1956, his chances of surviving numbered few. Jeffrey entered the room cautiously, unseen. He hesitated for a moment, weighing the consequences of saving the life of the one person who actually put Project Chronos into action. Quickly, he made his decision The time had arrived to test the effects of the time travel through Dr. Calendar's portal. Jeffrey stood over the Senator, arms outstretched. At first slowly and then more rapidly, he felt the Senator's life force enter his own body. Jeffrey turned and left the lifeless body.

No sooner than he exited the room and began to head down the corridor, Jeffrey heard the sound of footsteps rapidly approaching and then overtaking him. A doctor and a nurse ran into Dr. Calendar's room. Jeffrey stood at the door, observing as they began checking the oxygen. In a moment, they both rushed out. Jeffrey strode in, approaching Dr. Calendar as he gasped for breath. Jeffrey debated for one last second. Then, deftly, he tore off the oxygen tent. Standing over Dr. Calendar, Jeffrey placed his hand on his chest. Dr. Calendar awoke suddenly. The familiar whirring sound filled the air, along with the familiar blue light. The life force flowed back into Dr. Calendar. In a few short moments, he sat up, renewed with vitality. Jeffrey smiled at him.

"Well, there's proof that your work does serve a noble purpose," Jeffrey took Dr. Calendar's hand.

"I owe you my life, sir," Dr. Calendar's eyes glowed in amazement.

"Come on. Let's get you out of here before anyone suspects anything," Jeffrey reached for Dr. Calendar's clothes and tossed them onto the bed.

They discreetly shuffled down the hall and retrieved Jen and Jason.

"We'll explain later. Let's go, quickly," Jeffrey urged them.

They quickly barreled down the back steps to avoid detection. Once in the brisk night air, they hustled away from the hospital property. A few blocks away they boarded the bus to nearby Westfield.

Fifteen minutes later, Jeffrey, Jen, Jason and Dr. Calendar disembarked from the bus. Dr. Calendar strode around the corner to the taxi service's tiny storefront and requested a cab. In less than five minutes, they rushed into the Calendar mansion. Peering around, they noticed the nondescript black car parked across the street. They had company—uninvited guests.

"Get to the study. Fire up the portal. I will return and set the date. Let me distract them first," Dr. Calendar urged.

The FBI men quietly left their car and proceeded to walk up the long driveway, shrouded in darkness. Dr. Calendar flipped the switch to the outside light, waiting at the door to greet them.

"You're not going anywhere—and neither are your guests," the first agent drew his handgun, waving it at Dr. Calendar.

"Now, a bit more civility would help, gentlemen. After all, we are on the same team, aren't we—or are we? I do sometimes wonder," Dr. Calendar motioned them to come in.

"Just wait right here and I shall produce my house guests for you," Dr. Calendar turned on his heels and proceeded briskly to the study.

Deftly, he flipped the toggle switches on the machine and set the knob well ahead to 2016. The familiar whirring began and the blue fog once again enveloped the room.

Chapter VIII

2016

As the blue fog lifted, the Clymans gasped for breath. Each time they exited the portal, the side effects seemed to grow stronger. Jeffrey held onto Jen and Jason tightly. The dizziness gripped them until they could hardly stand up. Daylight began to break. One by one, they stood up and surveyed the scene. True to form, the portal had deposited them farther down the road. The familiar white church overlooking the pond greeted them with the tolling of its bells, as it had for over two hundred years. A powerful sun rapidly cast the shadow of the church spire, as if pointing the way for the Clyman family. They ambled up onto the gazebo, peering around. At first glance, not much appeared to have changed.

The crackle of a police radio startled Jeffrey, Jen and Jason. They swung around to see two officers exiting the parked patrol car, approaching them. They had forgotten that the police station lay adjacent to the park. In the pond, they saw the reflection of the flashing lights.

"Don't move," the voice commanded.

"Are you armed?" the other voice, a female voice, inquired.

Jeffrey shook his head. Both officers approached the Clymans cautiously, their hands resting on their weapons.

"You can't sleep in the park. Now, move out," the male voice barked.

The Clymans descended from the gazebo nodding and left promptly. Jeffrey led them down the block, turned the corner and stopped in a parking lot behind the row of stores. They needed a game plan.

"Dad, why are we here?" Jason's tone became anxious.

"Now we think we know how the soul switchers got started, who's involved and what motivated them. Next, we need to find out just how far they got with their plan, and whether it took any turns or stayed on track," Jeffrey explained in hushed tones, glancing around.

They stood just yards away from the spot where the election campaign parade passed them sixty years earlier. The irony struck Jen first.

"Jeffrey, so far everything we know has come from Dr. Calendar. But he could be dead by now. How do we find out what's going on without raising any suspicion?" Jen asked.

"Did you notice that we haven't seen any news stands or any telephone booths? And did you notice those cameras mounted on the wall of the building as we came around the corner? It's all about the technology now. I suspect computers are pretty much running nearly everything. So, we need to get access to one, in order to learn more," Jeffrey suggested.

"And you have a plan to do that, I supposed?" Jen folded her arms, with discontent across her face.

"I'm working on it; I'm working on it," Jeffrey reassured them.

"I'm getting hungry," Jason grumbled.

"I suppose you'll work on that, too," Jen remarked.

"Patience, patience, my dears," Jeffrey soothed their fears.

Before they could take another step, the two uniformed officers approached them again, this time withdrawing their weapons.

"You'll have to come with us," barked the male officer.

"No, they won't. They'll come with me," a familiar voice rang out behind them.

They turned on their heels, stirring up dust and gravel, surprised to see John Calendar himself. He pointed to the limousine.

"Get in."

Jeffrey, Jen and Jason studied John Calendar, looking for any sign of emotion. They found none. Slowly, as the police departed in the patrol car, the Clymans climbed into the back seat of the limo. John Calendar took the front seat, next to the driver. The doors slammed shut. The door locks clicked. The dark tinted window separating front and back seats rose up. It felt like a prison cell.

The car rolled out of the parking lot. The Clyman family members glanced out of the rear window. No one in sight. Their uneasiness grew. Jason whispered.

"I don't like him. How could you work for him? I'm still hungry. He's gonna die today any way. I know it."

Jeffrey and Jen sat on either side of Jason, each placing an arm on his shoulder, forming a protective cocoon. They knew about his ability. He never made a mistake with his predictions, ever since childhood. That's why the soul switchers abducted him. They all remained silent for the remainder of the short ride to the Calendar mansion. As they pulled into the driveway, Jeffrey peered around, expecting to perhaps see the FBI men again. No sign of them.

"Let's go," John Calendar stood by the back door of the limo as the driver opened it.

They followed him into the familiar site. Something felt different. Jeffrey, Jen and Jason all perceived it. They couldn't tell what—they just knew something had changed. John Calendar gestured for them to enter the residence. Reluctantly, each sensing the other's trepidation, they entered. The Clymans looked around. Jason picked it up first.

"I don't like that smell," he waved his arms.

Silently, they followed John Calendar down the hallway past the great room to the familiar study where they sat years before with his father. To them, it felt like only days, even hours since they left. They never quite recovered from the surreal quality of it all. John Calendar walked behind the desk, gesturing for the Clymans to take the chairs. He maintained his characteristic stance—arms behind his back, hands clasped together. He seemed to look *through* them rather than *at* them. John Calendar turned to face Jeffrey, staring down at him.

"I told you when the time was right, all would be revealed to you. Your impatience will unravel your life—first slowly, then more rapidly. Now, what have you learned about us in all of your travels?"

Jeffrey arose from his chair, circling the desk. Jen and Jason watched with amazement. The two men sparred like court room adversaries. Jeffrey placed his hands on the back of Jen's chair, leaning over her shoulder.

"And what return favor will you promise for the knowledge we've gathered?"

John Calendar snorted.

"How do I know you have anything worth sharing? And what assurance do I have that you're even telling the truth?"

Jeffrey straightened up, approaching John Calendar. The two men stood face to face.

"That's a chance you'll have to take."

Jason began to fidget in his chair, his hunger and his boredom overtaking him. Jeffrey glared back at John Calendar, speaking slowly and deliberately.

"What's to stop me from taking my family and returning through the portal right back to where we started?"

John Calendar smirked, dismissing Jeffrey with a wave of his hand.

"Everything. Technology has changed the world. It's not the world you left behind. We've even changed how the portal works. Now you need access."

Jeffrey nodded, conceding the point. Jason shifted in his chair again, then addressed Jeffrey.

"Why can't we just go home, dad, and forget all this? I want to go home now. We have to go."

John Calendar sat on the edge of his desk, leaning first in Jason's direction, then pivoting over to Jeffrey as he responded.

"You can't go home. Your home is gone. You've been away so long your home has gone into foreclosure. You have no home."

Jason became agitated. Red-faced, he scowled and jumped up from his chair, facing John Calendar.

"You are an evil person. And you are going to die TODAY!"

John Calendar tilted his head back, roaring with laughter.

"Doubtful, son. Highly doubtful."

Then John Calendar turned to face Jeffrey again.

"And if I did die, Project Chronos would go on without me. You see, that's the beauty of it all. We designed the program to perpetuate itself. Besides, why resist when you know we will produce a favorable outcome? We will prevail and we will maintain the balance this world so desperately needs."

"And just what balance is that?" Jeffrey glared at him.

"I think you know by now, but it bears repeating. We have staved off the scourges of the unclean souls that would trample on your very own values. We have set the ball in motion to rid the world of those who would drag us down, squandering their lives and our resources.

Think of it—no more need to house and feed the addict, the smoker, the self-indulgent, undisciplined obese; we can now redirect our time, attention and finances to build a more productive society."

Jeffrey circled the desk stealthily, like the jackal stalking his prey.

"You sound the same as every other self-righteous megalomaniac. So noble, oh so noble. And you sir—your arrogance will be *your* undoing. Did you ever think there might actually be a higher power—something bigger than us that determines those forces? Perhaps you are destroying the balance of nature rather than maintaining it. Did you ever consider that we are on this earth to care for one another—to deal with the wrongs of society, not to eliminate them?"

John Calendar once again tilted his head back and let out a laugh.

"So, you just became a man of faith? You're going to ply me with religion? Religion hasn't solved any of the world's ills for centuries. It's time to let science do the job now. More people have died in religious wars that didn't deserve to. Perhaps you think the Inquisition was just? Or the Salem witch trials? You're a bright man, Jeffrey. You still have time to rethink this."

Jeffrey first faced his family members, as if they were the court room audience. Slowly, he spun around to face John Calendar.

"And what about the holocaust? Did six million Jews deserve to die because one man decreed it? Do you call that 'science'?"

Jen and Jason began to feed off of Jeffrey's renewed energy. John Calendar pointed to the chair, gesturing to Jeffrey to sit down as he took his place behind the desk. Then he slid a drawer open on the desk and deftly began to press buttons. The wooden panels on the wall behind him retreated, revealing a series of screens. Each came to life as John Calendar pressed the keys on his keyboard. Each depicted a live video with subtitles in different languages superimposed across the bottom. John Calendar swiveled around in his chair, pointing to each of the screens as he spoke.

"We've gone international now, Mr. Clyman. We have a presence in nearly every country of the civilized world. Behold: China, Russia, Korea, Japan, The United Kingdom, France, Spain, Italy. And we're making a similar impact to what you have witnessed here in the U.S. Take a look. Soon we will spawn a whole new generation that will no longer need to concern itself with pampering those who throw away the precious gift of life."

Jeffrey nodded, acknowledging but not agreeing with John Calendar. The argument had all the trappings of genuine concern for the future welfare of humanity—or did it? Jeffrey mused to himself before gesturing broadly to John Calendar.

"Suppose your plan succeeds. How do we know that it won't result in enslaving humanity? Or diminishing the next generation's ability to solve other problems for itself when they arise?"

John Calendar once again slowly arose from his desk, leaning forward as he addressed Jeffrey.

"Mr. Clyman, I believe I taught you well. I admire your concern—and your sincerity. I know it's well placed. However, your premise is flawed. History has taught us over and over again that morality does not drive our life force—expediency does. Unfortunately, the human race does not have enough time to wait for everyone to fall into line. That's where *we* come in. I know you saved my father's life."

Jeffrey smiled, thinking perhaps he had finally struck a nerve in the iron clad persona he knew so well. Wrong again. John Calendar smirked, then addressed Jeffrey coldly.

"I'm sorry you did that. He was a miserable S.O.B. His only valuable contribution was his work on Project Chronos. We buried him last year, in case you're wondering."

Jeffrey shook his head in disbelief, that even John Calendar, who professed to place a high value on human life above all else, could remain so callous. John Calendar stood up behind the desk, leaned over and pressed one more button on his keyboard. An even larger screen lit up, dominating the wall behind him. He pointed to it confidently as the images began to take shape. Jeffrey, Jen and Jason became transfixed as John Calendar began to speak.

"And now, you are about to witness the event we have all been waiting for—the culmination of our hard work. Behold! You see here assembled in this arena, a phalanx of soul switchers. We are preparing to martial our forces and combine our collective strength to effect the first ever mass soul switching—remotely. That's right, we will extract the life force of an entire group of the undeserving and infuse it into the bodies of an entire facility full of hand picked terminally ill patients. Exciting? I call it an unprecedented scientific breakthrough."

Jeffrey, Jen and Jason glanced furtively at one another, then once again fixed their eyes on the large screen. They watched the phalanx of soul switchers as they stood in a circle, joined hands and slowly raised their arms. The familiar blue fog began to envelop them, obscuring each person one by one. The characteristic whirring built to a deafening crescendo. A flash of blinding light filled the room. The screen burst into fragments, sending glass flying. Jeffrey leapt out of his chair, throwing Jen and Jason to the floor, shielding them with his own body. In the melee, they could hear an agonizing wail. Jeffrey peered up as the room grew silent. John Calendar lay on the floor, his body riddled with fragments of glass. Jeffrey crawled over to him. Blood trickled from John Calendar's nose, mouth and eyes. His voice crackled.

"We've done it. We succeeded."

Jeffrey attempted to drag John Calendar; he resisted, waving his arms as he spoke.

"Get to the portal. Take your family to safety. The code is in my desk drawer."

Once again, Jeffrey hesitated only for a moment of indecision. Then he spoke.

"Come with us. We'll get you help."

John Calendar clutched his throat. Jeffrey watched the blood pour out of an open wound as the man spoke his final words and took what might be his last breath.

"It's too late. Go now."

Jeffrey leaned over Jen and Jason, helping them up. The smoke began to dissipate as the three Clyman family members opened the bookcase wall and entered the portal.

Chapter IX

1936

The blue fog slowly dissipated into a thin vapor, then disappeared, revealing the three Clyman family members. They each took a deep breath, holding on to one another. Something seemed amiss. The characteristic dizziness enveloped them. Jason spoke first.

"Dad, we're still here. We didn't go anywhere. Maybe they broke the machine. What's going on?"

Jeffrey put his finger to his lips and whispered.

"Shhh. Listen. I hear voices. It sounds like a radio broadcast."

Jeffrey put his ear to the wall. The voice continued.

"Today, Allied troops began a sweep of several European cities and small villages. The President has authorized further deployments in an effort to maintain control of the region. In a radio address last night, he calmed the fears of the American public when he promised to quell the rising forces of Communism, Nazism and Fascism that plague our allies. He pledged the full support of the United States. Here at home, women have been signing up to help pack provisions for our soldiers. At this time, we will pause for our national anthem before signing off for the night. We wish all of our listeners a safe, healthy 1936."

Jeffrey whispered to Jen and to Jason.

"Strange; we thought Dr. Calendar invented the portal in 1946. Maybe this was an earlier version of the machine. Maybe it's not as powerful. Could be that's why we are still inside the house this time. Shhh. I hear someone coming. Stay quiet."

Jeffrey could hear two voices. He instantly recognized one. The other had a distinct foreign accent.

"Dad, what's that gibberish?" Jason asked.

"It's not gibberish; it's German, son. I can pick out a little from what I learned in high school. Let's hope they switch to English soon," Jeffrey answered.

"Herr Doctor Calendar, I haff placed myself at great risk to shteal the plans for zis machine from ze Germans. As I haff told you, zey vere going to use ze portal to invade ze United Shtates. I am relying on you to honor our agreement and get me paid by your government," the German demanded.

"Yes, yes, Sigmund, I know. We haven't forgotten you. We appreciate your sacrifice. We will reward you as promised. We just need to conduct a few more tests. You do realize, of course, that this is merely a prototype that we built from the plans. We may have to make certain refinements for the portal to work properly. Rest assured, as soon as we know the machine will perform as expected, we will get you the remainder of your payment. Now, if you will excuse me, I have a lot of work to do. The sooner I can verify that the machine works, the sooner we can get you paid and on your way," Dr. Calendar replied.

Jeffrey turned to Jen and to Jason.

"So, Dr. Calendar didn't invent the machine; he just perfected it. That explains a lot."

"What do we do now, dad?" Jason asked nervously.

"We wait. We wait until the coast is clear. We still need to find out who is really running the show—who started this whole thing," Jeffrey whispered to Jen and to Jason.

Jeffrey pressed his ear against the bookcase again, listening intently. The lone muffled voice continued.

"Julius Calendar here. Get me the Director. Tell him it's important. Yes, I'll wait, but not long."

Jeffrey could only hear one end of what he surmised was a telephone conversation. The voice became more and more agitated.

"I haven't got all day. He can call me back. What kind of an operation are you running there, anyway? Calendar. Dr. Julius Calendar. C-A-L-E-N-D-A-R. Yes, of course he has the number."

Jeffrey motioned to Jen and Jason to keep still and to remain silent. The air behind the library bookcase grew stale. The accumulated dust on the books began to penetrate their nasal passages. Jeffrey feared one of them might sneeze and give away their position. What seemed like a half hour passed as they remained crouching silently. Suddenly, they all snapped to attention as the distinct sound of a ringing telephone broke the silence. Jeffrey resumed his stance by the bookcase. He could hear Dr. Calendar's voice ring out.

"Mr. Director, our man has delivered as promised, and we have built and tested the machine based on the plans he procured. We need to get him paid and get him out of here before the Germans suspect anything. I'm sure you know how serious a situation we have on our hands if he should become disgruntled and word got out. Certainly, it's become a matter of national security. We knew from the start what we had gotten into. At least this places us on an equal footing with the Germans. Exactly what do you mean when you say, 'your people will take care of it?' Of course, it became my problem. So, you'll provide protection for me? Do I have your word on that? Very well then. We will proceed with the experiments and report back to you shortly," Dr. Calendar responded, in his usual gruff manner.

Jeffrey struggled to hold back a cough as the dry dusty air settled in his throat. He continued to press his ear to the library wall as another dialog began.

"Rollins, I'm going out for a short while. As you know, our guests will begin arriving soon. Make sure the Mrs. has whatever she needs—and that she has arranged for someone to look after the tot during tonight's gala."

"I presume you are referring to your son, sir?"

"Of course, I am. Someone has to keep the little bastard quiet. And I'll not reward you for a flippant attitude. Maintain your demeanor."

"Sir, Mrs. Calendar has been unwell. Are you sure she should entertain guests this evening?"

"She will do as I tell her to do. Now, carry on, Rollins."

"As you wish, sir."

Jeffrey, Jen and Jason huddled in the corner behind the bookcase, beginning to tire. After a while, they began to hear the distant sound of voices down the corridor, presumably in the great room. Then, Jeffrey heard the study door open. He resumed his position by the bookcase. He could hear the voices of a man and a woman.

"Dr. Calendar, do you think we should—here, now? Aren't you worried that Mrs. Calendar might find us?"

"Come here. There now, sit on the desk. Doesn't that feel good?"

Jason and Jen could now discern the dialog as the volume of the voices elevated with their excitement. Jason whispered.

"Dad, are they doing it? You know, sex?"

"Shhh; not yet" Jeffrey cautioned.

"Drop your drawers, Trudy," the voice commanded.

"I don't think we should—ooh..."

"You may call me Julius, my dear. Now, assume the position."

Jeffrey turned to Jen and Jason, nodding his head.

"It looks like the Professor has his hands full," Jeffrey whispered.

The woman giggled and left soon after. Jeffrey could hear Dr. Calendar pacing around the room. Another voice, another conversation soon ensued.

"We have been authorized to award you an extension to your grant, provided you expedite the modifications to the machine and demonstrate to our satisfaction that it will perform as desired," the other voice rang out clearly.

"Of course, it will perform as promised, just as soon as I complete the work. Do you have the bank draft in your possession?" Dr. Calendar demanded.

"We will deliver it by courier as soon as you complete the demonstration. The Director himself has assured me of this. Your government thanks you, " the other voice insisted.

"Does the Vice-President know yet? Has the Director informed him of our progress?" Dr. Calendar queried.

"He personally authorized the operation and the funds. Hereafter, we will refer to the program as 'Project Chronos,' " the other voice stated.

"Very well, then. You will hear from me as soon as we are prepared to conduct the demonstration," Dr. Calendar replied.

Jeffrey turned to Jen and Jason, whispering.

"This goes even higher than we imagined. Now we know what we need to know. So, this all began as a cloak and dagger espionage operation with the intention of getting on an equal footing with our enemies. I doubt they had any idea where it would go. It appears they only knew about the portal as a means of time travel. I don't think they learned about the soul switching until later."

"Yeah; when they took me away," Jason answered.

"It would appear so," Jeffrey acknowledged.

"So, now we know Dr. Calendar acted on orders," Jen added.

"And let's not forget; he was really a paid operative, lining his own pockets—not to mention a philanderer," Jeffrey asserted.

"Where to, now for us?" Jen asked nervously.

"We have to sit tight and wait—at least until Dr. Calendar's guests have left. I'm not sure how this ancient version of the portal even works," Jeffrey shook his head.

"Then we might as well just get some rest. We all need it," Jen motioned for Jeffrey and Jason to lie on the floor. As Jason lay across her lap, his eyes began to close. Jeffrey succumbed, sliding down to a sitting position and leaning against Jen's shoulder. The heaviness of the day overcame him, and he too began to lapse into a deep sleep.

The room swirled around; then it became round. All three Clymans sat up with a start. They found themselves in caskets, placed in a circle. A blinding whiteness enveloped them. They began to stretch their arms out—suddenly, Jeffrey sprang up, landing against the bookcase wall. The dream ended. The force of his collision with the wall knocked several books on the other side to the floor with a crash. Jeffrey hoped nobody heard it.

The muffled sound of a telephone ringing broke the silence again. Jeffrey resumed his stance, ear to the wall. He recognized Dr. Calendar's voice.

"Sigmund, is that you? Yes, of course I received confirmation of the payment in advance of our conversation—and again, from the highest level. I can personally assure you of that. I'm expecting it to arrive any time now. I will call you as soon as it—what? You're threatening me? Why, this is outrageous! It's nothing more than blackmail. You're doubling your price? Or what, sir? You'll tip off the Germans that we have the plans to the portal? I thought you were an honest—they did what? Sent two agents to kill you? I had nothing whatsoever to do with any such thing. And I swear to you I knew nothing about it. Sigmund, Sigmund. What was that noise? Are you there?" Dr. Calendar nearly dropped the phone, storming out of the room.

Jeffrey waited. No more sounds. Then, uncontrollably, the dust finally got to him He sneezed so violently he fell against the bookcase wall, pushing it open a crack. Slowly, it opened, revealing the whole Clyman family. Rollins the butler snorted at Jeffrey.

"Wherever you came from, I suggest you return without incident."

Rollins closed the bookcase wall and strode out of the room. Jeffrey could hear Dr. Calendar call to him from the corridor.

"Rollins, is everything all right?"

"Just rats sir—just rats. I took care of them," Rollins replied.

Jeffrey woke Jen and Jason.

"Time to go. I'll fill you in later."

He began to fiddle with the knobs and the dials on the ancient machine, not entirely sure where it would take them. He pressed the levers forward all the way, hoping to go as far into the future as possible. The familiar whirring began; the blue fog descended on the Clymans as they all held on to one another. It felt strangely different this time.

Chapter X

2026

The usual dizziness overcame Jeffrey, Jen and Jason, accompanied by nausea. Choking back the rising water in their throats, they reeled and fell against the library door. It opened. They each darted a furtive glance around the study. Immediately they noticed the Calendar mansion stood in a state of disrepair. They struggled to regain their balance, choking on the dusty air. A distant voice penetrated the silence. They recognized it. As they quietly approached the door, they saw Rollins the butler. He appeared disheveled and disoriented. Rollins shuffled down the corridor, approaching the study. He mumbled. The Clymans stood behind the door, listening.

"I went through the portal. I didn't want to. I had to. They would have taken me...potato chips. Chipping the golf ball. Poker chips. Chip off the old block. Chipped tooth. I'm not chipped. I don't want to be chipped."

Jeffrey, Jen and Jason eyed one another quizzically as Rollins passed the study, still mumbling to himself. As he disappeared around a corner, they slipped out, heading for the front door. As they navigated the corridor, they noticed the burned-out light bulbs, the cracked plaster, the thick layer of dust that pervaded the once elegant mansion.

The Clymans made their way down the street, noticing that several of the formerly exquisite homes appeared deserted. Suddenly, they all felt a rush of air as a deafening sound rocked the quiet of the small town. An aircraft like nothing they had ever seen whizzed by at an uncomfortably low altitude. Jeffrey, Jen and Jason grabbed onto one another, rattled by the aircraft. As quickly as it passed them, it took a hairpin turn, heading for them. Once directly overhead, it abruptly stopped, hovering over them. A warm sensation bathed them as a faint pink beam of light hit them. A mechanical voice demanded an answer.

"State your business."

Jeffrey replied instantly in an equally mechanical fashion.

"We-are-going-to-the-library."

As quickly as it came, the craft raced away, lights flashing.

"I'm guessing that's the new police force," Jeffrey volunteered.

The Clymans continued the walk into town, noticing the changes along the way. Tired and hungry, they couldn't help but remark on how few people they encountered. Fortunately, the library had moved across the street from its original headquarters in the municipal building. All the better to avoid any further police contact. The automatic door swung open. Jeffrey reasoned it must have sensors activating it. Entering the library, the Clymans experienced a form of culture shock. They saw no books, no magazines, no microfilm readers—nothing familiar at all. They sheepishly approached a young woman behind a wraparound console with recessed screens. She raised her eyes without lifting her head. Passing her hand over one of the screens, she spoke.

"How may I assist you today?"

Jeffrey responded in like manner, quietly.

"Is there by any chance a computer here that I could access?"

The young lady slowly straightened up to her full towering height, answering Jeffrey.

"Chip, please."

Jeffrey's quizzical expression alerted her. She held out her arm, displaying an implanted microchip. Jeffrey shook his head. She motioned for them to follow her down a corridor and behind a row of old-style library shelves, known in the Clymans' time as "the stacks." The young lady placed her finger to her lips and spoke in hushed tones.

"Most everyone has been micro-chipped. Only those in the resistance or the outlying regions have not. So, you must be from one or the other. The cameras are nearly everywhere. The micro-chips monitor our vital signs, our speech, our movements and even our thoughts. Then they transmit them back through the cameras to the High Command. This section is one of the only areas not secured. We maintain it for those patrons who have not been fixed. I see by your confusion that you do not understand. The soul switchers control everything, including reproduction. Those who have not been fixed and still have sexual urges come here to perform. Now, we must go. Here, take this. You will need it to access the computer over in that corner."

She handed Jeffrey a crystal as she hastened back to her station at the console. Jeffrey, Jen and Jason all eyed one another curiously as they proceeded to the corner with the computer. Jeffrey inserted the crystal. The familiar whirring sound kicked up as a blue light emanated from the screen. Jeffrey touched it. The keyboard appeared on the screen. Jeffrey punched in the one word, "Resistance." In a flash, a three-dimensional video began to play, depicting a battle between a small, ragged group and a phalanx of uniformed officers in riot gear. It took only seconds before the resistance evaporated in a beam of blue light. No blood. Just gone. Jeffrey gently touched the screen again. Another three-dimensional video began to play. This one appeared like a newscast, recounting a series of events about the resistance. The spokesman stood up from behind his console and approached the wall-sized monitor. Jeffrey, Jen and Jason became fixated as the action unfolded. Dressed in old style camouflage, a resistance leader urged action. His face obscured and his voice disguised, he invited anyone seeing the broadcast to join in the fight against the repression. The spokesman began to interact with him in interview fashion, asking him to enumerate the casualties and the losses his movement had suffered. The resistance leader reached back and pulled a woman into view. She leaned forward and removed her hat, exposing a shaven head covered with scars and lacerations. Slowly, she raised both of her arms, extending them out from the sleeves of her jacket. She had no hands. A bright flash of light filled the screen. The news spokesman fell to the floor as the walls of the studio collapsed. Crew members dropped to the floor one by one until the last camera operator fell. The transmission ended abruptly. The screen went blank.

Jeffrey teared up, unable to hold back his pervasive grief. Jen wrapped her arms around him. Jason sobbed profusely. Jeffrey reached over and touched the screen again. Another video opened up, this time in the old two-dimensional style of old. The news spokesman pointed to a series of still photos appearing on a large video screen. Jen pointed to one of the photos.

"Can you freeze it?"

Jeffrey tapped the screen twice. The image froze. Jen turned to Jeffrey, pointing to a figure in the background.

"There. Isn't that Francisco Torres?"

Jeffrey squinted, surveying the image.

"Yes. I worked with him at the law firm. That's our entree. If he's still alive and if we can find him. Come on. Let's go. I think I know where to look," Jeffrey shut down the computer and removed the crystal, slipping it into his pocket.

The Clymans quickly left the library.

"I don't even know if they still have buses or trains around here," Jeffrey shook his head.

A warm sun blasted through the cloud cover, penetrating the haze. Jeffrey led the way down the quiet tree-lined side streets, not wanting to draw attention to them. Strangely, they did not see a soul in sight—no cars, no pedestrians. Finally, they crossed the town line into the borough of Clarksville. Jeffrey took a left turn at the main intersection of the tiny town. Working their way behind a row of boarded up stores, Jeffrey instructed them to climb over the piles of tires. They found themselves at the back of the old, abandoned bowling alley. Surveying the scene, they came upon a lone dog, tied to a fence. The dog reared up cautiously. Jeffrey approached, equally cautious. Before they could move, a net fell over them from above. Two figures dressed in camouflage slid down ropes from the roof of the bowling alley. They circled the Clymans, sizing them up. One of them spoke from behind his mask.

"You got weapons? You armed? Who are you?"

Jeffrey answered.

"No weapons. A friend of Francisco Torres. Is he here?"

The second figure, a woman poked at Jeffrey through the net.

"Who wants to know?"

"Tell him, Jeffrey Clyman. We used to work together."

The man in camouflage responded.

"Are any of you chipped?"

Jeffrey, Jen and Jason rolled up their sleeves to reveal their arms.

"No chips; no weapons. Tell Francisco Jeffrey wants to see him."

The woman leaned in to the net.

"We don't take orders from you."

The man waved her away.

"Take them inside. We'll check them for weapons; then we'll cut the net if they're clean."

The man opened the rusted old metal door to the back of the bowling alley. Inside, the darkness obscured everything. The man reached over, turning a bulb in a wall socket. The door slammed shut behind them. The woman patted each of the Clymans down.

"They're clean," she announced.

The man withdrew a hunting knife from the sheath on his belt, slicing the net off of them. He turned his back; the woman rested her hand on the grip of a pistol holstered at her waist. The man removed his mask, turning around to face the Clymans.

"Francisco! You son of a gun! So, it was you," Jeffrey exclaimed.

Francisco laughed, then embraced Jeffrey.

"You can never be too careful today. You could have been a soul switcher," Francisco cleared his throat.

"It's been a long time, my friend", Jeffrey eyed the scars on Francisco's forearms.

"Sit. Have some water. You look worse than I do," Francisco studied Jeffrey.

"We've been through a lot—but not as much as you," Jeffrey confided.

"I remember your wife. I never met your son. Sorry it has to be under these conditions. Bimbo, watch the door, please. We call her that, but she is anything but—smart, sexy and ruthless...everything a man could want," Francisco laughed.

"It would take too long to tell you everything we've learned. It looks like things have gone from bad to worse here. We've just been trying to trace this thing from the beginning and follow the trail to see where it goes. I guess you know John Calendar died. We saw it happen. So, do you know who's running the show?" Jeffrey probed gently.

"No. If we knew that, we would have had them by now. We know this thing goes way high up the food chain, but how high—nobody seems to know," Francisco shook his head, removed his bandana and wiped his forehead.

Jeffrey surveyed the room.

"They can't hear you?"

"Lead, baby; we lined the place with lead. My mom didn't raise no fool," Francisco slapped Jeffrey on the back.

"More fun than practicing law, eh?" Jeffrey smirked.

"Now there is only one law—the law of survival. They think they've got everyone under their thumb. We've got plans, too...and guns," Francisco's face morphed into a serious stare.

"So, how can we help?" Jeffrey asked.

"I thought you'd never ask. We have a fundraiser scheduled—an art exhibit to draw out some of the upper crust. We figure if they've still got money, they've got to be connected to the soul switchers. If we can get them in one place, we can blow them away," Francisco pounded his fist on the table.

Jen and Jason appeared visibly shaken. Francisco eyed them.

"They can stay here. You can come along—if you can handle one of these," Francisco slid a handgun over to Jeffrey.

Jeffrey could hardly believe what he had heard. He glanced over at Jen, who had turned away, and nodded to Francisco.

"I'm in," he consented.

Jason leaned in to Jen and whispered.

"He's not going to make it. He's not coming back. I know it. I know it. He's not."

Jen hoped that no one heard him. She knew if he felt it, it always came to pass.

The air inside the old bowling alley had become stale. As night fell, the Clymans felt stifled. They longed to breathe the night air. Bimbo stood guard at the door for hours, never appearing to tire. Jen attempted to have a conversation with her. To no avail; she answered in monosyllables. Jason had fallen asleep on the floor, in the corner. Jeffrey and Francisco readied themselves for the next day's activity. They could hear a gentle rain tap the metal roof. Gradually, the intensity of the rain increased until it pounded and gushed off onto the sidewalk. Eventually, it seeped under the door. Bimbo sloshed it around with her military issue boots. Jeffrey and Jen longed to experience the smell of the rain on the pavement. Not safe. Then the jets streamed overhead, too close for comfort. The search lights illuminated the whole property. No one moved.

Jeffrey, Jen and Jason awoke to the clang of the metal door opening. Bright sunlight stabbed their eyes. The smell of bacon frying permeated the room, wafting over them. Francisco tended to the small stove as Bimbo jumped, sliding from a rope on the roof, landing in the doorway. Jeffrey sized her up. Short, compact and sinewy. She bent over to lace up her boots; her breasts heaved as she grabbed an overhead water pipe and began to do pull-ups. Jen shot Jeffrey a knowing look. He took the hint and dropped into a chair at the table as Francisco served up his makeshift breakfast. They all ate in silence, anticipating the events of the day.

"We're going in as the catering crew. We're meeting a contingent on arrival at eleven hundred hours. We'll enter through the back door. Keep your weapons concealed at all times. We can't afford any mistakes. On my signal, we waste every guest. We need to make a statement here. I've got press people tipped off. We need to show our strength," Francisco gave orders like a seasoned officer to his troops.

They piled into the rusty old Jeep, Bimbo at the wheel, Jeffrey in the back and Francisco concealing their arsenal in the heated food boxes. Pulling into the heart of Westfield, they parked behind the art gallery just as the well to do patrons began to arrive. A trio played music, oblivious to their plans. The patrons began to sample the fare in the chafing dishes. The gallery curator droned on, extolling the virtues of the exhibit. Sunlight poured into the room. Suddenly, without warning, before anyone could react, police in riot gear crashed through the wall and began firing their laser weapons. Patrons fell one by one, smoke pouring from their wounds. Francisco, Jeffrey and Bimbo dove for cover. They were outgunned. The room fell silent; bodies piled everywhere. A lone reporter captured the scene with his camera before falling to the floor as the last shot took him down—after he hit the "send" button and uploaded his story.

Francisco limped, then fell forward, clutching his chest. The shot proved fatal. Jeffrey lay on top of Bimbo in an effort to protect her.

"Well, how do they feel?" She laughed, sliding his hands off of her breasts.

Embarrassed, Jeffrey smiled at her.

"Looks like you enjoyed it," she giggled, noticing his arousal.

"I guess we both did. That will have to remain our secret," Jeffrey cautiously raised himself up on one knee, checking the room.

"Somebody compromised our operation. The soul switchers knew we were coming. They pulled off the massacre to blame it on the resistance," Bimbo stood up like someone who lost a baseball game rather than a friend and companion.

"Get undressed," she commanded, slipping out of her jumpsuit.

"What?" replied a stunned Jeffrey.

"You have to get out of those clothes. Take some from one of the stiffs. The soul switchers use scent tracking," she related.

"Dogs?" Jeffrey asked as he quickly undressed.

"Electronic. Ten times more powerful," Bimbo answered.

They grabbed their weapons, hopped into Francisco's Jeep and headed back to the bowling alley. Jeffrey drove, his eyes fixated cautiously in the rear-view mirror. Bimbo leaned her head on his shoulder. Slowly, she began to run her fingers playfully up and down Jeffrey's leg. He did not react. Instead, he turned to address her.

"Weren't you and Francisco an item?"

"Yeah, in the beginning. Then he became all business—totally focused on 'the cause', as he called it. Everything changed. But we needed each other," Bimbo showed the first sign of a break in that wall she erected around herself as her voice cracked and she nearly teared up.

"What's your story? What made you like this?" Jeffrey asked, with full sincerity.

Bimbo stared out the windshield, then slid down in the seat, responding mechanically.

"I had a twin sister. She had special abilities; you know—like your son. They came for her one day—the soul switchers. They took her away. She refused to play their game. They returned her, but she was never the same. We had to put her in that halfway house—Devonshire. I went to visit her one day and found her hanging from a pipe by a bed sheet. It really messed me up."

"Was here name Hannah, by any chance?"

"Yeah. How did you know?" Bimbo leaned in, squinting her eyes at Jeffrey.

"My son Jason was there. He knew her. In fact, he was very fond of her. Please—you can't tell him. He would go to pieces. He's not that strong," Jeffrey implored her.

"Yeah; I get it. No worries. One more secret between us, right?" Bimbo poked Jeffrey in the ribs.

When they arrived back at the bowling alley, they announced themselves, Jen let them in, securing the door after them. Jeffrey's face told the story. Jen threw her arms around his neck. Jason nodded; he knew. Bimbo took charge of the room.

"I know why you're here. I'll tell you what you want to know so you can leave. There's nobody in charge. It's all automated. That's right. No chief soul switcher."

Bimbo marched towards the bathroom and began undressing.

"I'm taking a shower. Anyone want to join me? Can the modesty; there's not much hot water."

Just as she was about to slip out of her underwear, Jen grabbed a tablecloth, came up behind her and threw it over her.

"My son doesn't need to see this—and neither does my husband," she seethed.

Bimbo turned her back, letting the cloth fall and waltzed into the shower. No one followed her. When she emerged, she dried off and donned a pair of cargo pants and a camouflage shirt. She tossed the keys to the Jeep at Jeffrey.

"Take it. Leave it by the cemetery gate and walk to the Calendar mansion. I'll retrieve it later, when things settle down," Bimbo advised.

Jen and Jason unlocked the door and exited the building, heading for the Jeep. Jeffrey turned to Jen.

"Let me say goodbye. She's had a rough time. I'll be right out," Jeffrey assured Jen.

Jen eyed him suspiciously as he closed the heavy metal door with the familiar clang.

Jeffrey turned to face Bimbo. He leaned down toward her, intending to kiss her on the forehead. Before he had a chance, she jumped up, wrapped her legs around him, kissed him squarely on the lips and thrust her tongue into his mouth. At the same moment, she ground her crotch against him. He could feel the heat. Jeffrey disengaged and turned toward the door.

"It's Alice. My name is Alice," Bimbo shouted at him.

"Goodbye, Alice," Jeffrey strode out the door and slammed it shut behind him. In silence, he climbed into the Jeep and turned the key, his eyes fixed on the road as he left the bowling alley parking lot.

Jason seemed especially agitated during the ride, keeping watch out the rear window of the Jeep. Jeffrey killed the headlights in an effort to remain inconspicuous. Jen leaned her head back, exhausted from worry. Jeffrey stayed on as many back roads as he could to avoid detection. Only one of the super jets streaked overhead, its bright spotlight scanning and narrowly missing them.

Finally, they parked the Jeep and walked up the long driveway of the Calendar estate. No apparent signs of life. As they approached, Jeffrey noticed the front door appeared ajar. He jumped in front of Jen and Jason protectively. He pushed the door open with one quick motion, then stood back. One lone light bulb flickered inside. Jeffrey leaned in, then motioned for Jen and Jason to follow. They traversed the familiar hallway toward the study. Not a sound. Peering into the dark room, Jeffrey motioned for Jen and Jason to follow. No sooner than he set foot in the room, he nearly tripped over something. He bent down to find the lifeless body of Rollins the butler. Jeffrey reached for a wall switch. Dried blood pooled next to Rollins, his face battered. Jeffrey leaned over him. No pulse. He signaled to the others to open the bookcase panel as he approached the controls for the portal. At that very moment, as he fired up the portal, he heard the sound of heavy foot falls down the corridor. The familiar whirring sound kicked up; the blue light poured out; Jeffrey lunged into the portal, joining Jen and Jason. Jason looked at him in disbelief.

"Are we really going home, dad?"

"Yes, son. We're going home," Jeffrey assured him.

The police troopers appeared too late. The Clymans were gone. The commander nodded. One officer ignited his flame thrower, setting the study ablaze. The smell of burning books filled the air. Immediately, the room became enveloped in a cloud of white. The flames disappeared; smoke choked the soul switchers police. In an instant, a high-powered hose knocked them off their feet. Alice and her band of rebels snatched up the officers' weapons, ran out the door and hopped on to the vintage fire truck as the hose retracted, careening down the road.

Jeffrey, Jen and Jason stood on their doorstep for the first time in what seemed like an eternity. Everything remained exactly as they left it. Still, Jeffrey cautiously inserted the key in the door, peering in to investigate. All quiet. The Clymans closed the door behind them and dropped into their living room easy chairs. It all seemed so strange—like a dream or a trance. They decided to go out to eat the first real dinner they had in—well, years. They agreed not to discuss the events of their travels with anyone.

Upon their return, they still felt their experiences had a surreal quality—as though they were not sure it all really happened. The time travel proved wearisome, to say the least. They felt displaced in their own universe. After a short rest, Jeffrey stoked up the fireplace. An hour later, Jeffrey doused the coals. They all agreed they needed sleep. Jason stood behind Jen, his hands on her shoulders as he spoke.

"Mom, dad, can I stay here? I don't want to go back to the halfway house—not yet anyway."

Jeffrey, knowing what Alice had told him, agreed.

"Sure, son. That would probably be the best thing," Jeffrey assured him.

The familiar sounds of the neighborhood at night crept in. Cats meowed; dogs barked; an owl hooted; the breeze stirred the dried leaves swirling across the Clymans' front lawn. All seemed peaceful. The magic of sleep wafted over each of them, cleansing their anxieties. No one stirred. Jeffrey held Jen in his arms.

The morning sun pierced the shades in the master bedroom. Jen awoke slowly, still feeling the blissfulness of a good night's sleep. She turned to face Jeffrey; his side of the bed was empty. She arose, donning her bath robe. Throwing cool water on her face, Jen brushed the hair out of her eyes. Next, she headed for the kitchen, expecting to find Jeffrey at the table. No Jeffrey. Her heart sank as she picked up the folded piece of paper and read the note to herself.

"Dearest Jen and Jason,

Please know that I love you both more than anything or anyone on this earth. Please also know that with the knowledge we now possess, it is incumbent upon us to fight the evil that corrupted a once noble mission. I must go back. I beg of you to do whatever you can to quietly begin to plant the seeds of resistance before this thing gains the momentum we have seen. Most of all, stay close to members of the press. They are our only salvation. I will return—when my work is done.

Jeffrey"

Jen nearly collapsed into a kitchen chair, both crying and praying at the same time. A few miles away, Jeffrey reached into his pocket, fingering the crystal as he drove up the long driveway of the Calendar estate.

* * *

*Watch for **Return to Soul Switchers**, the next chapter in the continuing Soul Switchers saga. Visit: www.Soulswitchers.us*

For sales, editorial information, subsidiary rights information or a catalog, please write or phone or e-mail
AbsolutelyAmazingEbooks
Manhanset House
Shelter Island Hts., New York 11965, US
Tel: 212-427-7139
www.BrickTowerPress.com
bricktower@aol.com
www.IngramContent.com

For sales in the UK and Europe please contact our distributor,
Gazelle Book Services
White Cross Mills
Lancaster, LA1 4XS, UK
Tel: (01524) 68765 Fax: (01524) 63232
email: jacky@gazellebooks.co.uk

CPSIA information can be obtained
at www.ICGtesting.com
Printed in the USA
JSHW031148190822
29481JS00007B/239

9 781955 036337